VICTORIA MARY SACKVILLE

(1892–1962) was born at Knole in Sevenoaks, Kent. Her parents were first cousins, her father being the third Baron Sackville and her mother the illegitimate daughter of Lionel Sackville-West and the Spanish dancer Pepita. Knole was to be an abiding passion throughout her life, the inspiration of much of her writing, and the source of great sorrow when, as a woman, she was unable to inherit it on her father's death. Vita was educated at home, except for three years spent at a school in London where she came to know Violet Keppel (later Trefusis) with whom, from 1918–21, she was to have a passionate affair.

In 1910 Vita met Harold Nicolson, the young diplomat whom she married three years later. In 1915 they bought a cottage two miles from Knole where they planned their first garden; three years later Vita Sackville-West's first novel, *Heritage*, was published. A distinguished novelist, poet, short-story writer, biographer, travel writer, critic, historian and gardener, her novels include *The Edwardians* (1930), *All Passion Spent* (1931) and *Seducers in Ecuador* (1942); of her poetry, *The Land* (1926) was awarded the Hawthornden Prize and *The Garden* (1946) won the Heinemann Prize.

During the 1920s her close and influential friendship with Virginia Woolf was at its height, culminating in the publication of Virginia Woolf's novel *Orlando* (1928), a celebration of her friend. In 1930 Harold and Vita bought Sissinghurst Castle in Kent, where they created their famous garden. A Fellow of the Royal Society of Literature and a JP for Kent, Vita Sackville-West was made a Companion of Honour in 1948. She died at Sissinghurst, after an operation for cancer, at the age of seventy.

Virago publishes *The Edwardians, All Passion Spent, Family History* (1932), *No Signposts in the Sea* (1961) and *Seducers in Ecuador & The Heir* (1922).

VIRAGO
MODERN
CLASSIC

NUMBER
269

Vita Sackville-West

SEDUCERS
IN ECUADOR
&
THE HEIR

WITH A NEW INTRODUCTION BY
LISA ST AUBIN DE TERÁN

Virago

Published by VIRAGO PRESS Limited 1987
41 William IV Street, London WC2N 4DB

Seducers in Ecuador first published in Great Britain by
Leonard and Virginia Woolf at The Hogarth Press 1924
Copyright Vita Sackville-West 1924
The Heir first published in Great Britain by
Wm. Heinemann 1922
Copyright Vita Sackville-West 1922

This edition first published in Great Britain by
Virago Press 1987
Introduction © Lisa St Aubin de Terán 1987

British Library Cataloguing in Publication Data

Sackville-West, V.
  Seducers in Ecuador; and The heir. ——
  (Virago modern classics).
  I. Title   II. Sackville-West, V.   The heir
  823'.912 [F]   PR6037.A35

ISBN 0-86068-772-4

Typeset by Goodfellow & Egan Ltd. of Cambridge
Printed in Great Britain by
Cox & Wyman Ltd. of Reading, Berkshire

INTRODUCTION

The name of Vita Sackville-West is well known for many reasons, ranging from notorious scandals to exquisite gardens, and from famous court cases to the authorship of poetry and prose. Born in 1892, she was the daughter of two cousins, Lionel Sackville-West and Victoria, an exotic despotic woman with a strain of Spanish gipsy in her veins. Their daughter, an only child, grew up at Knole, the family seat, and the largest house in England, spanning four acres with its halls and corridors. Here she developed an intense love of places, of buildings, of things. She lived in the rarified atmosphere of the English aristocracy before the Great War, thriving on the luxuriant mixture of excessive attention and comparative neglect.

When her father died, she, the presumed heiress of Knole, that adored Elizabethan palace that had been in the Sackville family for so long, was passed over in favour of a male cousin. Her sense of identity seemed to go with her birthright. Had she been a boy, Knole would have been hers. Perhaps much of her subsequent sexual ambiguity stemmed from that twist of fate. Even as a child, she must have known that she was really expected to have been a boy.

Meanwhile, Vita sunk her house-passions, albeit vicariously, in a villa in Constantinople, and then in her English Long Barn where she lived with her husband, Harold Nicolson. They had met at a dinner party in 1910, and they married in 1913. Their life together was a tapestry of tempestuous episodes interlaced with years of calm. They shared each other, with varying degrees of resistance, with many others, but her most intense love affair was with Violet Trefusis (née Keppel). This was a love begun in childhood that was to rage and wane for much of her adult life. However, Harold Nicolson's biographer, James Lee-Milne, has written that it was

"Vita's deep atavistic love of Knole which Harold had to understand was the really serious rival he had to face".

Many of her other friendships were passions, and many of her passions were later distilled into friendship. Virginia Woolf, who was once (literally) Vita's lover, wrote her novel *Orlando* as a tribute to Vita Sackville-West and to the dream house of her childhood, Knole.

The two short novels in this volume were also written as tributes: *The Heir* was a homage and a farewell to Knole, and *Seducers in Ecuador* was an offering to Virginia Woolf. The latter was written while Vita and Harold were on holiday in the Dolomites in July 1924. She wrote from there to Virginia Woolf in England "you asked me to write a story for you on the peaks of mountains and beside green lakes I am writing it for you".

Superficially, the two stories would seem very different, both in their subject matter and their style. And yet, they are both tales of chivalry, both improbable in their plots, and both heavily allegorical. *Seducers in Ecuador* is a short ironic fantasy wherein the hero, or rather, anti-hero, Arthur Lomax wages a Quixotic and sadly destructive battle to behave well and honourably. Like a fly, he enmeshes himself further and further into the web of intrigue and deceit that surrounds him. The story begins in Egypt, and adopting the fashion of the times there, Lomax takes to wearing blue spectacles. From the moment he dons these protective lenses, his whole perception of the world is altered, not only is he shielded from the sun, but from reality as well. Each character in the tale lives in a world of their own fantasy, and Lomax manages to stumble into most of them, wreaking a trail of desolation born entirely of his good intentions.

The Heir, written two years earlier, is clearly deeply rooted in Vita's own background. Although the house that she describes with such tender detail is not literally Knole, the feelings there stem directly from her own knowledge and love of country houses and their power to bind those who live in them. *The Heir* is subtitled *A Love Story*, and it describes the awakening of true love in the heart of Peregrine Chase upon his arrival at the Elizabethan Manor house of his old aunt. She has died and is lying in state upstairs, while the greedy estate agent and executor wait below to carve up the property that the dull young nephew has inherited. Chase initially finds the house dusty and its attractions veiled, but his senses gradually keen to his surroundings. The house devours and calms all his anxieties. The gardens, the peacocks, the servants and furniture and even the greyhound Thane, flesh out from their first introduction as liabilities into bastions of all that is good and pure of traditional values. The tenants welcome him, the dog pines for him and the once "ghostly" garden fruits as luxuriantly as the spilling out of a cornucopia. Amongst so much fertility the house itself is eroticised into a sensual woman. "Blackboys", as the house is called "laid the hands more gentle and more detaining than the hands of any woman about his heart".

Greed and modern times, the urge to destroy the past, then enters into unarmed combat, as it were, with Chase who is "poor and hard working in a cheerless fashion; he managed a branch of a small insurance company in Wolverhampton and expected nothing further out of life". Without the aid of any coloured spectacles, Chase's vision of the world is altered. He arrives to dispose of his unwanted inheritance and he quite simply falls in love with it, echoing more suddenly, but in many ways, closely, Vita's own love of place and property. There is no element of commercial interest here, or pleasure at a "good investment", this is the love of sacrifice, a preservation of beauty, a championing of the weak by the strong. Chase, who enters the story as a hopeless wimp is transformed into a strong man by his quest, but although he becomes the master of his own emotions, "the centre of all was always the house, that mothered the farms and accepted the homage of the garden. The house was the heart of all things."

Paradoxically, Peregrine Chase sees Eden (Blackboys) itself as the snake, since it stirs feelings and responsibilies that threaten the anonymity of his dreary life. The story unfolds with a constant spur of suspense: will Chase bite the apple and taste the fruits of paradise, or will he sell up and return to his office in Wolverhampton? Will he save the tenants from eviction? Will the beautiful peacocks who roam the grounds be put down? Will the hoards of sightseers buy his house when it is put up for auction? Or will it be the symbolic Saracens: the exotic, bejewelled and decadent Brazilians who have their eye on Blackboys? Chase is defending the old world from the new. He is not just "Fighting for his house? No, No! more, far more than that: fighting for the thing he loved. Fighting to shield from rape the thing he loved." Vita Sackville-West has made of this simple tale a medieval romance and a chivalric adventure. There are ingredients of a challenge by a mysterious opponent, a love quest, and the seduction of the knight by the bewitching temptress. However, Chase (whose name suggests chastity, an essential value for a knight), has no white charger and no funds to save his metaphorical castle, nor has he, at least to start with, the usual attributes of an Arthur or a Launcelot.

The theme of *The Heir* is one of nostalgia for a passing England and dissolving values, it is at once both a celebration and an invitation to mourn the loss of a great house and the unchanging values that remain cocooned within it.

Given the author's almost obsessive love for houses, *The Heir* is a much more sincere book than the apparently flippant *Seducers in Ecuador*. Neither of these stories are particularly significant in the context of her writing as a whole. Compared to *All Passion Spent* or *The Edwardians* or her long poem, *The Land* or her journals, they carry much less weight. And yet, they are both interesting and, each in its own way, unique. The one becoming a testimony of her greatest love and frustration, and the other being a metaphorical view of the author's own strange predicament. The preposterous plot of *Seducers in Ecuador* with its hanging of a man for a crime that was not a crime and the scapegoating of Lomax, the anti-hero, also has roots in Vita Sackville-West's own life. Arthur Lomax puts on a pair of glasses and finds that the whole world becomes "more than curious; it was magical". With his eyes shielded, "his common sense was divinely in abeyance; and he kept it that way". Lomax ventures in and out of the real world by the device of his coloured lenses, experimenting in all the colours, thus making the world of fantasy and make-believe become the real world, at least for him.

There is no evidence that Vita was addicted to dark glasses, though many people subsequently have hidden behind them, but, by donning male attire and, sometimes, changing her name to "Julian", Vita used to step out of her persona as chatelaine, wife, mother of two sons, landscape gardener, novelist and respected member of a coterie of writers centring around the Bloomsbury set, and become the scandalous, often fleeing, lover of the ever ready and equally brilliant Violet Trefusis. Sometimes the two personae of Vita Sackville-West sat side by side, particularly in later years when she became more settled into Sissinghurst, the now National Trust house that she restored with Harold Nicolson and where she lived and gardened. Sometimes, though, she would just run away, often to the continent, to live a life of decadence and romance and disrepute. She had her own brand of coloured spectacles to put on whenever her world became inexplicable or even just dull. Whatever it was that ruled the phases of her life, shifting as she did from one gear to the next so readily, it must have fascinated her to create a character who could (and by a much more socially acceptable means) change his identity and the role of everyone around him.

Seducers in Ecuador is like a challenge to the reader. It doesn't unfold its plot, as such, it blurts it out right at the beginning. Early on in the story the author teases "the practised reader will have observed by now that the element of surprise is not to be looked for in this story". It is a challenge to know all but still read on. However many twists and turns the story takes, there are, despite the above quotation, many surprises. However, misfortune sits so heavily on the shoulders of Arthur Lomax that, by the end, one is scarcely surprised at anything that befalls him, except, perhaps, to marvel that he was not also drawn and quartered after his hanging. Nothing is real or stable in this story, the ground shifts constantly under the readers feet and the rules are forever being reinvented.

Lomax, sailing on a yacht with a party of weird and uncommunicative guests is ensnared by a Miss Whitaker, a woman who would have the world, and particularly Lomax, believe that she has been seduced by a dashing bounder who has fled to Ecuador. Lomax marries her, believing her to be pregnant and in distress. His chivalrous move merely begins a chain reaction of calamities, and all for nothing, because Miss Whitaker is neither in distress nor pregnant, she merely writes letters to an imaginary lover in South America. Oddly, by the end of the book, the one truly believable character is the missing cad in Ecuador.

This ironic downfall of a successful man who insists on wearing shades and becomes one of life's failures, was well received when it was first published. Virginia Woolf commented in a letter to Vita when she first received the manuscript "I'm certain that you've done something much more interesting (to me, at least) than you've yet done . . . I'm very glad we're going to publish it." The other members of the Bloomsbury set also approved of Vita's new book, though Virginia Woolf was probably less pleased to see that in America, when her *Mrs Dalloway* was reviewed on the same page as *Seducers in Ecuador*, it was Vita's book that got the top space and the better review of the two.

Vita herself once wrote to her friend Eddie Marsh that she had written *Seducers in Ecuador* as a joke. Perhaps it doesn't matter what an author's motives are on writing a book, all that matters is the end product. And, as Vita says herself, commenting on Lomax's trial, "how pitiable a weapon was truth—individual fantasy was the only potent defence".

Arthur Lomax went to the scaffold. Vita Sackville-West lived on at Sissinghurst in Kent where she died in 1962.

Lisa St Aubin de Terán, Legnaro, Italy, 1987

SEDUCERS
IN ECUADOR

TO
VIRGINIA WOOLF

SEDUCERS IN ECUADOR

It was in Egypt that Arthur Lomax contracted the habit which, after a pleasantly varied career, brought him finally to the scaffold.

In Egypt most tourists wear blue spectacles. Arthur Lomax followed this prudent if unbecoming fashion. In the company of three people he scarcely knew, but into whose intimacy he had been forced by the exigencies of yachting; straddling his long legs across a donkey; attired in a suit of white ducks, a solar topee on his head, his blue spectacles on his nose, he contemplated the Sphinx. But Lomax was less interested in the Sphinx than in the phenomenon produced by the wearing of those coloured glasses. In fact, he had already dismissed the Sphinx as a most overrated object, which, deprived of the snobbishness of legend to help it out, would have little chance of luring the traveller over fifteen hundred miles of land and sea to Egypt. But, as so often happens, although disappointed in one quarter he had been richly and unexpectedly rewarded in another. The world was changed for him, and, had he but known it, the whole of his future altered, by those two circles of blue glass. Unfortunately one does not recognise the turning-point of one's future until one's future has become one's past.

Whether he pushed the glasses up on to his forehead, and looked out from underneath them, or slid them down to the tip of his nose, and looked out above them, he confronted unaided the too realistic glare of the Egyptian sun. When, however, he readjusted them to the place where they were intended to be worn, he immediately re-entered the curious world so recently become his own. It was more than curious; it was magical. A thick green light shrouded everything, the sort of light that might be the forerunner of some undreamed-of storm, or hang between a dying sun and a dead world.

He wondered at the poverty of the common imagination, which degraded blue glasses into a prosaic, even a comic, thing. He resolved, however, not to initiate a soul into his discovery. To those blessed with perception, let perception remain sacred, but let the obtuse dwell for ever in their darkness.

But for Bellamy, Lomax would not have been in Egypt at all. Bellamy owned the yacht. A tall, cadaverous man, with a dark skin, white hair, and pale blue eyes, he belonged to Lomax's club. They had never taken any notice of one another beyond a nod. Then one evening Bellamy, sitting next to Lomax at dinner, mentioned that he was sailing next day for Egypt. He was greatly put out because his third guest, a man, had failed him. "Family ties," he grumbled; and then, to Lomax, "somehow you don't look as though you had any." "I haven't," said Lomax. "Lucky man," grumbled Bellamy. "No," said Lomax, "not so much lucky as wise. A man isn't born with wife and children, and if he acquires them he has only himself to blame." This appeared to amuse Bellamy, especially coming from Lomax, who was habitually taciturn, and he said, "That being so, you'd better come along to Egypt to-morrow." "Thanks," said Lomax, "I will."

This trip would serve to pass the time. A yachting trip was a pleasant, civilised thing to undertake, and Lomax appreciated pleasant, civilised things. He had very little use for the conspicuous or the arresting. Such inclinations as he had towards the finer gestures— and it is not to be denied that such inclinations were latent in him—had been judiciously repressed, until Lomax could congratulate himself on having achieved the comfortable ideal of all true Englishmen. From this trip, then, he anticipated nothing but six or seven agreeable weeks of sight-seeing in company as civilised as his own. It is, however, the purpose of this story to demonstrate the danger of becoming involved in the lives of others without having previously tested the harmlessness of those others, and the danger above all of contracting in middle-age a new habit liable to release those lions of folly which prowl about our depths, and which it is the duty of every citizen to keep securely caged.

Of course one cannot blame Lomax. He knew nothing of Bellamy, and for Miss Whitaker his original feeling was one of purely chivalrous compassion. Besides, it must be remembered that under the new influence of his spectacles he was living in a condition of ecstasy—a breathless condition, in which he was hurried along by his instincts, and precipitated into compromising himself before he had had time to remove his spectacles and consult his reason. Indeed, with a rapidity that he was never well able to understand, he found himself in such a position that he no longer dared to remove his spectacles at all; he could not face a return to the daylight mood; realism was no longer for him. And the spectacles, having once made him their slave, served him well. They altered the world in the most extraordinary way. The general light was green instead of yellow, the sky and the desert both turned green, reds became purple, greens were almost black. It produced an effect of stillness, everything seemed muffled. The noises of the world lost their significance. Everything became at once intensified and remote. Lomax found it decidedly more interesting than the sights of Egypt. The sights of Egypt were a fact, having a material reality, but here was a phenomenon that presented life under a new aspect. Lomax knew well enough that to present life under a new aspect is the beginning and probably also the end of genius; it is therefore no wonder that his discovery produced in him so profound and sensational an excitement. His companions thought him silent; they thought him even a little dull. But they were by that time accustomed to his silence; they no longer regarded him as a possible stimulant; they regarded him merely as a fixture— uncommunicative, but emanating an agreeable if undefined sense of security. Although they could not expect to be amused by him, in each one of them dwelt an unphrased conviction that Lomax was a man to be depended upon in the event of trouble. The extent to which he could be depended upon they had yet to learn.

It is now time to be a little more explicit on the question of the companions of Lomax.

Perhaps Miss Whitaker deserves precedence, since it was she, after all, who married Lomax.

And perhaps Bellamy should come next, since it was he, after all, for whose murder Lomax was hanged.

And perhaps Artivale should come third, since it was to him, after all, that Lomax bequeathed his, that is to say Bellamy's, fortune.

The practised reader will have observed by now that the element of surprise is not to be looked for in this story.

"Lord Carnarvon would be alive to-day if he had not interfered with the Tomb," said Miss Whitaker to Lomax.

Lomax, lying in a deck-chair in the verandah of their hotel, expressed dissent.

"I *know* it," said Miss Whitaker with extreme simplicity.

"Now how do you know it?" said Lomax, bored.

But Miss Whitaker never condescended to the direct explanation. She preferred to suggest reserves of information too recondite to be imparted. She had, too, that peculiarly irritating habit of a constant and oblique reference to absent friends, which makes present company feel excluded, insignificant, unadventurous and contemptible. "*You and I* would never agree on those questions," she replied on this occasion.

Lomax asked her once where she lived in London. She looked at him mistrustfully, like a little brown animal that fears to be enticed into a trap, and replied that she was to be found at a variety of addresses. "Not that *you'd* find me there," she added, with a laugh. Lomax knew that she did not mean to be rude, but only interesting. He was not interested; not interested enough even to ask Bellamy. Bellamy, now, interested him a great deal, though he would always have waited for Bellamy to take the first step towards a closer intimacy. Bellamy, however, showed no disposition to take it. He was civil and hospitable to his guests, but as aloof as a peak. Lomax knew him to be very rich and very delicate, and that was about the sum of his knowledge. Bellamy's reticence made his confidences, when they did finally come, all the more surprising.

Artivale, the fourth member of the party, was on the contrary as expansive as he well could be. He was a dark, slim, poor, untidy young scientist, consumed by a burning zest for life and his profession. His youth, his zeal, and his ability were his outstanding characteristics. Bellamy in his discreet way would smile at his exuberance, but everybody liked Artivale except Miss Whitaker, who said he was a bounder. Miss Whitaker admired only one type of man, and dismissed as perverts or bounders all those who did not belong to it; which was unfortunate for Lomax, Bellamy, and Artivale, none of whom conformed. Her friends, she let it be understood, were men of a very different stamp. Artivale did not appear to suffer under her disapprobation, and his manner towards her remained as candid and as engaging as towards everybody else, no less sure of his welcome than a puppy or a child. With him alone Lomax might have shared the delight of the coloured spectacles, had he felt any desire so to share. Artivale had skirted the subject; he had settled his spectacles, peered about him, and laughed. "By Jove, what a queer world! Every value altered." He dashed off to other trains of thought—he couldn't stay long poised on any one thing,—giving Lomax just a second in which to appreciate the exactness of his observation.

Artivale was like that—swift and exact; and always uninsistent.

Lomax went to the chemist in Cairo, and bought all the coloured spectacles he could find. He had already his blue pair, bought in London; in Cairo he bought an amber pair, and a green, and a black. He amused himself by wearing them turn and turn about; but soon it ceased to be an amusement and became an obsession—a vice. Bellamy with his reserve, and Heaven knows what tragedy at the back of it; a finished life, Bellamy's, one felt, without knowing why. Miss Whitaker with her elaborate mystery; an empty life, one felt, at the back of it; empty as a sail inflated by wind—and how the sails bellied white, across the blue Mediterranean! Artivale with his energy; a bursting life, one felt, thank God, beside the other two. Lomax with his spectacles. All self-sufficient, and thereby severed from one another. Lomax thought himself the least apart, because, through his glasses, he surveyed.

He was wearing the black ones when he came on Miss Whitaker sobbing in the verandah.

Miss Whitaker had not taken much notice of him on the journey out. She had not, in fact, taken much notice of anybody, but had spent her time writing letters, which were afterwards left about in subtle places, addressed to Ecuador. Arrived in Egypt, she had emerged from her epistolary seclusion. Perhaps it had not aroused the comment she hoped for. She had then taken up Lomax, and dealt out to him the fragments of her soul. She would not give him her address in London, but she would give him snippets of her spiritual experience. Allusive they were, rather than explicit; chucked at him, with a sort of contempt, as though he were not worthy to receive them, but as though an inner pressure compelled their expectoration. Lomax, drunk behind his wall of coloured glass, played up to the impression he was expected to glean. He knew already—and his glasses deepened the knowledge—that life was a business that had to be got through; nor did he see any reason, in his disheartened way, why Bellamy's queer yachting party shouldn't enrich his ennui as far as possible.

He was, then, wearing his black spectacles when he came on Miss Whitaker sobbing in the verandah.

The black ones were, at the moment, his favourites. You know the lull that comes over the world at the hour of solar eclipse? How the birds themselves cease to sing, and go to roost? How the very leaves on the trees become still and metallic? How the heaven turns to copper? How the stars come out, terrible in the day-time, with the clock at mid-day instead of at midnight? How all is hushed before the superstition of impending disaster? So, at will, was it with Lomax. But Miss Whitaker, for once, was a natural woman.

"Oh," she said, looking up at last, "do for goodness' sake take off those horrid spectacles."

Lomax realised then the gulf between himself, dwelling in his strange world, and the rest of mankind in a wholesome day. But he knew that if he took them off, Miss Whitaker would immediately become intolerable.

"The glare hurts my eyes," he said. So do we lie. Miss Whitaker little knew what she gained. Looking at Lomax, she saw a man made absurd. Looking at Miss Whitaker, Lomax saw a woman in distress. All womanhood in distress; all womanhood pressed by catastrophe. His common sense was divinely in abeyance; and he kept it there. What else, indeed, was worth while?

To Miss Whitaker, too, was communicated a certain imminence. Her own stories were marvellously coming true. Indeed, to her, they were always true; what else was worth while? But that the truth of fact should corroborate the truth of imagination! Her heart beat. She kept her eyes averted from Lomax; it was her only chance. He kept his eyes bent upon her; it was his. At all costs she must not see the glasses, and at all costs he must see through them, and through them alone. He gazed. The chair she sat was a smoky cloud; her fragility was duskily tinged. Her tears were Ethiopian jewels; black pearls; grief in mourning. Yet Lomax had been, once, an ordinary man, getting through life; not more cynical than most. An ordinary man, with nothing in the world to keep him busy. Perhaps that had been his trouble. Anyway, that was, now, extravagantly remedied.

It took a long time to get a confession out of Miss Whitaker. She could write Ecuador on an envelope, and without comment allow it to be observed, but she could not bring herself to utter so precise a geographical statement. There were moments when it seemed to Lomax, even behind the black glasses, perfectly ridiculous that he should suggest marriage to Miss Whitaker. He did not even know her; but then, certainly, the idea of marriage with a woman one did not know had always appeared to him a degree less grotesque than the reverse. The only woman in his life being inaccessible, one reason for marriage with anybody else was as good as another. And what better reason than that one had found a lonely woman in tears, and had looked on her through coloured glasses?

Miss Whitaker knew only that she must keep her head. She had not thought that the loose strands cast by her about Lomax could have hardened so suddenly into a knot. She had never known them so harden before. But what an extraordinary man! Having spent her life in the hopes of coming across somebody who would play up, she was astonished now that she had found him. He was too good to be believed in. Very rapidly—for he was pressing her—she must make up her mind. The situation could not be allowed to fritter out into the commonplace. It did not occur to her that the truth was as likely to increase his attention as any fiction. She was not alone in this; for who stands back to perceive the pattern made by their own lives? They plaster on every sort of colour, which in due time flakes off and discovers the design beneath. Miss Whitaker only plastered her colour a little thicker than most. She was finding, however, that Lomax had got hold of her paint-brush and was putting in every kind of chiaroscuro while she, helplessly, looked on. Now it was the grey of disillusion, now the high light of faith. The picture shaped itself under her eyes. She tried to direct him, but he had bolted with her. "Ten days ago", she tried to say, "you didn't know me." And, to make matters more disconcerting, Lomax himself was evidently in some great distress. He seemed to be impelled by some inner fire to pronounce the words he was pronouncing; to be abandoning all egoism under the exaltation of self-sacrifice. The absurd creature believed in his mission. And Miss Whitaker was not slow to kindle at his flame. They were both caught up, now, in their own drama. Intent, he urged details from her, and with now a sigh escaping her, and now a little flare of pride, she hinted confirmation. It was really admirable, the background which between them they contrived to build up; personalities emerged, three-dimensional; Ecuador fell into its place with a click. Even the expedition to Egypt fitted in—Miss Whitaker had accepted Bellamy's invitation in order to escape the vigilance of a brother. He had a hot temper, this brother—Robert; any affront to his sister, and he would be flying off to Ecuador. Robert was immensely wealthy; he owned an oil-field in Persia; he would spare no expense in searching Ecuador from end to end. He had already been known to scour Russia to avenge a woman. By this time Lomax was himself ready to scour Ecuador. Miss Whitaker wavered; she relished the idea of a Lomax with smoking nostrils ransacking Central America, but on second thoughts she dissuaded him; she didn't want, she said, to send him to his death. Lomax had an idea that the man—still anonymous—would not prove so formidable. Miss Whitaker constructed him as very formidable indeed; one of the world's bad lots, but in every sense of the word irresistible. Lomax scorned the adjective; he had no use, he said, for bad lots so callous as to lay the sole burden of consequences upon the woman. He used a strong word. Miss Whitaker blinked. The men she admired did not use such words in the presence of women. Still, under the circumstances, she made no comment; she overlooked the irregularity. She merely put up a chiding finger; not a word of blame was to be uttered in her hearing.

"By the way," said Lomax, as they finally parted to dress for dinner, "perhaps you wouldn't mind telling me your Christian name?"

The hotel façade was a concrete wall pierced with windows; the rooms were square compartments enclosing single individuals. Sometimes they enclosed couples, linked together by convention or by lust. In either case the persons concerned were really quite separate, whether they wanted to be or whether they didn't. They had no choice in the matter. Boots and shoes stood outside the doors, in a row down the passage. The riding-boots of soldiers, tanned and spurred. High-heeled, strapped shoes of women. Sometimes two pairs stood side by side, right and proper, masculine and feminine; and this made the single pairs look forlorn. Surely, if they could have walked without feet in them, they would have edged together? The little Anglo-Egyptian wife of the colonel, carefully creaming her nose before powdering it, wished that that Mr. Bellamy, who looked so distinguished, would ask them down to his yacht at Alexandria. The colonel, in his shirt sleeves, wished only that his stud would go into his collar. Artivale, bending over a dead chameleon, slit up its belly neatly with his nail scissors. The little Swiss waiter in his cupboard of a bedroom saw the sweat from his forehead drip upon the floor as he pared away the corn upon his toe. He sat, unconsciously, in the attitude of the Tireur d'Epines. But Lomax and Miss Whitaker, on reaching their bedrooms, paused appalled at their own madness as the blessing of solitude enclosed them with the shutting of the door.

It is not really difficult to get a marriage licence. Besides, once one has committed oneself to a thing, pride forbids that one should draw back. Nevertheless, Lomax was married in his spectacles—the blue ones. Without them, he could not have gone through the ceremony. They walked home, when it was over, *via* the bazaars. They had to flatten themselves against the wall to let a string of camels go by. The din and shouting of the bazaar rose round them; Achmed Ali, with cheap carpets over his arm, displayed to Miss Whitaker his excellent teeth and his bad Assiout shawls; some one smashed a bottle of scent and its perfume rose up under their feet, like incense before a sacrifice. Still they made no reference to what had just taken place. It was in their covenant that no reference should be made, neither between one another, nor to any one else. Time enough for that, thought Lomax, an indeterminate number of months hence. That was Miss Whitaker's business. When she needed him, she had only to send him a message. In the meantime, Bellamy met them on the steps of the hotel, more genial than usual, for he had been talking to the colonel's wife and she had amused him—a transient amusement, but better than nothing to that sad man.

"Been sight-seeing?" he inquired; and then, as Miss Whitaker passed into the hotel, "It's really noble of you, my dear Lomax," he said, "to have taken Miss Whitaker off like that for a whole morning."

Marion Vane's husband died that afternoon. She had sat by his bedside trying loyally not to think that now she would be free to marry Lomax. She did not know where Lomax was, for they had long since settled that it was better for them not to communicate. He would see the death in the papers, of course, and perhaps he would write her a formal letter of condolence, but she knew she could trust him not to come near her until she sent for him. This was April; in October she would send. Then she was startled by a faint throaty sound, and saw that the fingers which had been picking the blankets were once convulsed, and then lay still.

The *Nereid* set sail from Alexandria two days later. Bellamy did not seem able to make up his mind where he wanted to go. Sicily was talked of, the Dalmatian coast, the Piraeus, and Constantinople. The others were quite passive under his vacillations. Now they were afloat, and had re-entered that self-contained little world which is in every ship at sea; temporary, but with so convincing an illusion of permanence; a world weighing so many tons, confined within a measure of so many paces, limited to a population of so many souls, a world at the same time restricted and limitless, here closely bound by the tiny compass of the ship, and there subject to no frontiers but those of the watery globe itself. In a ship at sea our land life slips away, and our existence fills with the new conditions. Moreover in a sailing ship the governing laws are few and simple; a mere question of elements. Bellamy was sailor enough—eccentric enough, said some—to despise auxiliary steam. Appreciative of caprice, in the wind he found a spirit capricious enough to satisfy his taste. In a calm he was patient, and in a storm amused, and for the rest he comported himself in this matter, as in all others (according to his set and general principle), as though he had the whole leisure of life before him.

No shore was visible, for Bellamy liked to keep the shore out of sight. It increased, he explained, not only the sense of space but also the sense of time. So they lounged along, having the coasts of Barbary somewhere over the horizon, and being pleasantly independent of century; indeed, the hours of their meals were of greater import to them than the interval elapsed since the birth of Christ. This, Bellamy said, was the wholesome attitude. Bellamy, in his courteous, sophisticated, and ironical way, was ever so slightly a tyrant. He did not dictate to them, but he suggested, not only where they should go, but also what they should think. It was very subtly done. There was not enough, not nearly enough, for them to resent; there was only enough to make them, sometimes, for a skimming moment, uneasy. What if Bellamy, when they wanted to go home, wouldn't go home? What if, from being a host, he should slide into being a jailer?

But in the meantime it was pleasant enough to cruise in the *Nereid*, lying in deck-chairs, while Bellamy, with his hand on the helm and the great blade of the mainsail above him, watched from under the peak of his cap, not them, but the sea.

Very blue it was too, and the *Nereid*, when she was not running before a fair wind on an even keel, lay over to the water, so low that now and then she shipped a gobbet of sea, only a thin little runnel that escaped at once through the open scuppers of the lee runner, in a hurry to get back to its element. Bellamy was bored by a fair wind; he hated the monotony of a day with the sheet out and the beautiful scooped shape of the spinnaker, and the crew asleep for'ard, since there was no handling of gear to keep them on the run. What he liked was a day with plenty of tacking, and then he would turn the mate or the captain off and take the wheel himself, and cry "Lee-o!" to the crew. And what pleased him even better was to catch the eye of the mate and give the order with only a nod of the head, so that his unwarned guests slithered across the deck as the ship went about, when he would laugh and apologise with perfect urbanity; but they noticed that next time he had the chance he did precisely the same thing again. "Bellamy likes teasing us," said Lomax, with a good deal of meaning in his tone. Bellamy did, even by so slight an irritation. And once he brought off a Dutchman's gybe, which nearly shot Lomax, who was lying asleep under the mizzen-boom, into the sea.

One sleeps a great part of the time on a yacht. Artivale fished, and dissected the fish he caught, so that a section of the deck was strewn with little ribs and spines. Lomax surveyed these through his spectacles. Artivale had long slim fingers, and he took up and set down the little bones, fitting them together, with the dexterity of a lace-maker among her bobbins. Tailor-wise he sat, his hair lifted by the wind, and sometimes he looked up with a full smile into the

disapproving face of Miss Whitaker. "Play spillikins, Miss Whitaker?" he asked, jumbling his fish bones all together into a heap.

Very blue and white it all was. Soft, immense white clouds floated,
and the sails were white, and Artivale's tiny graveyard, but the
scrubbed deck, which in Southampton Water had looked white, here
appeared pale yellow by contrast. The sails threw blue shadows. The
crew ran noiselessly on bare feet. "When shall we get there?" Lomax
wondered, but since he did not know where "there" was, and since
all the blueness and whiteness were to him overlaid as with the
angry cloud of an impending storm, he was content to hammock
himself passively in the amplitude of enveloping time. He was,
indeed, in no hurry, for his land-life, now withdrawn, had been
merely a thing to be got through; he had an idle curiosity to see what
was going to happen in these changed aeons that stretched before
him; nor did he know that Marion Vane's husband was dead. So he
lay in his deck-chair, speculating about Bellamy, watching Artivale,
aware of the parallel proximity of Miss Whitaker—who was his
wife—in *her* deck-chair, and occasionally, by way of refreshment,
turning his eyes behind their owlish spectacles over the expanse of
his lurid sea and sky.

What of it, anyway? There were quite a number of other
communities in the world beside this little community, microscopic
on the Mediterranean. Lomax saw the blue as it was not, the others
saw or thought they saw the blue as it was, but unless and until our
means of communication become more subtle than they at present
are, we cannot even be sure that our eyes see colours alike. How,
then, should we know one another? Lomax lived alone with his
secret, Bellamy with his; and as for Miss Whitaker, if Truth be
indeed accustomed to dwell at the bottom of a well, at the bottom of
Miss Whitaker's heart she must surely have found a dwelling suited
to her taste. Artivale, being a scientist intent upon a clue, probably
knew more of the secrets of life than the seamen who begot their
offspring in the rude old fashion, but it is to be doubted whether
even Artivale knew much that was worth knowing. He claimed to
have produced a tadpole by ectogenetic birth, but, having produced
it, he was quite unable to tell that tadpole whither it was going when
it inconsiderately died, and, moreover, as he himself observed, there
were tadpoles enough in the world already.

Volcanic islands began, pitting the sea; white towns and golden temples clung to a violet coast. Bellamy suggested to them that they did not want to land, a suggestion in which they acquiesced. They shared a strange disinclination to cross Bellamy. They were sailing now within a stone's throw of a wild, precipitous coast, their nights and their days boundaried by magnificent sunsets and splendid dawns. But for those, time did not exist. Geography did not exist either; Bellamy referred to Illyria, and they were content to leave it at that. It fitted in with the unreality of their voyage. There are paintings of ships setting sail into a haze of sunlight, ships full-rigged, broad-beamed, with tracery of rope, pushing off for the unknown, voyages to Cythera, misty and romantic; Lomax wore the amber spectacles, and saw a golden ship evanescent in golden air. Morning and evening flamed upon the sea; each day was a lagoon of blue. Islets and rocks stained the shield of water; mountains swept down and trod the sea; cities of Illyria rose upon the breast of the coastline; rose; drew near; and faded past. Venice and Byzantium in spire and cupola clashed the arms of peace for ever on the scene of their exploits. But towns were rare; they passed not more than one in every four-and-twenty hours. For the rest, they were alone with that piratical seaboard descending barbarously to the sea; never a hut, never a road, never a goat to hint at life, but caves and creeks running between the headlands, and sullen mountains like a barrier between the water and the inland tracts. The little ship sailed lonely beneath the peaks. Day after day she sailed, idly coasting Illyria, and Bellamy waited for the storm. "Treacherous waters," he had observed on entering them. Indeed it seemed incongruous that the sea should be so calm and the shore so wild. Day after day unbroken, with that angry coast always on their right hand and the placid sea on their left; day after day of leisure, with a wall of disaster banking higher and higher against them.

Those paintings of ships show the ship setting sail in fair weather; they never follow her into the turbulence of her adventure. Friends speed her with waving handkerchiefs, and turn away, and know nothing of her till a letter comes saying that she has arrived at her place of port. And, for the matter of that, the lives of friends touch here and there in the same fashion, and the gap over the interval is never bridged, knowledge being but a splintered mirror which shall never gather to a smooth and even surface.

The *Nereid*, then, with her living freight, saw the serenity of Illyria broken up into a night of anger, but the wives of the crew, lighting their lamps in brick cottages at Brightlingsea, knew nothing of it, and the wife of the captain writing to her aunt said, "Joe has a nice job with a gentleman name of Bellamy on a yorl in the Meddingterranean", and Marion Vane with an edging of white lawn to her mourning at neck and cuffs was vague to her trustee at dinner regarding the disposal of her country house, for she believed that this time next year she would be married to Lomax. The *Nereid* was not bread-beamed; she was slim as a hound, and it was not with a plebeian solidity but with an aristocratic mettle that she took the storm. Her canvas rapidly furled, she rode with bare masts crazily sawing the sky. Black ragged night enveloped her; the coast, although invisible, contributed to the tempest, throwing its boulders against the waves as the waves hurled themselves against its boulders. The little boat, a thing of naught, was battered at that meeting-place of enemies. Rain and spray drove together across the deck, as momently the storm increased and the wind tore howling through the naked spars. The men were black figures clinging to stays for support, going down with the ship when she swooped from the crest down into the trough, rising again with her, thankful to find the deck still there beneath their feet, lashed by the rain, blinded by the darkness, unable to see, able only to feel, whether with their hands that, wet and frozen, clung to rail and stanchion, or with their bodies that sank and rose, enduring the tremendous buffeting of the tossing ship, and the shock of water that, as it broke over the deck, knocked the breath from their lungs and all but swept them from their refuge into the hopeless broiling of the sea.

Lomax was in the deck-house. There, he was dry, and could prop himself to resist the rearing and plunging; and could almost enjoy, moreover, the drench of water flung against the little hutch, invisible, but mighty and audible, streaming away after sweeping the ship from end to end. A funny lot they would be to drown, he reflected; and he remembered their departure from Southampton, all a little shy and constrained, with Miss Whitaker sprightly but on the defensive. How long ago that was, he failed to calculate. They had drifted down to Calshot, anchoring there on a washed April evening, between a liquid sky and oily lagoon-like reaches, gulls and sea-planes skimming sea and heaven, in the immense primrose peace of sunset. And they had known nothing of one another, and Miss Whitaker had written letters after dinner in the saloon. Well, well! thought Lomax.

There came a fumbling at the deck-house door, a sudden blast of wind, a shower of spray, and Bellamy, in glistening oilskins, scrambled into the shelter, slamming the door behind him. A pool began to gather immediately round him on the floor. Lomax thought that he looked strangely triumphant,—as though this were his hour. "Glad to have got us all into this mess," he thought meanly. It aggravated him that he should never yet have found the key to Bellamy.

"I want to talk to you," cried Bellamy, rocking on his feet as he stood.

He wanted to talk. External danger, then, gave him internal courage.

"Come into my cabin," he cried to Lomax over his shoulder as he began to make his way down the companion.

But Lomax, really, knew nothing of all this. The storm, really, had not entered his consciousness at all; Bellamy, and Bellamy alone, had occupied it all the while. All that he knew, really, was that he found himself in Bellamy's cabin.

In Bellamy's cabin, everything loose had been stowed away, so that it was bare of personal possessions; the narrow bunk, the swinging lamp, the closed cupboards alone remained untouched in the cabin that had sheltered the privacy of Bellamy's midnight hours. Lomax, as he lurched in through the door and was violently thrown against the bunk, reflected that he had never before set foot in the owner's quarters. They were small, low, and seamanlike; no luxury of chintz softened the plain wooden fittings; Lomax forgot the delicate yacht, and saw himself only in the presence of a sailor aboard his vessel, for Bellamy in his sou'wester and streaming oilskins, straddling in sea-boots beneath the lamp, had more the aspect of a captain newly descended from the bridge than of the millionaire owner of a pleasure yawl. He kept his feet, too, in spite of the violent motion, while Lomax, clinging to the side of the bunk, could barely save himself from being flung again across the cabin.

But Bellamy stood there full of triumph, fully alive for the first time since Lomax had known him; his courteous languor dropped from him, he looked like a happy man. "This weather suits you," Lomax shouted above the din.

The yacht strained and creaked; now she lifted high on a wave, now fell sickeningly down into the trough. Water dashed against the closed port-hole and streamed past as the ship rose again to take the wave. Cast about in all directions, now dipping with her bows, now rolling heavily from furrow to furrow, she floundered with no direction and with no purpose other than to keep afloat; govern herself she could not, but maintain her hold on life she would. Lomax, who in the cabin down below could see nothing of the action of the sea, felt only the ship shaken in an angry hand, and heard the crash of tumult as the seas struck down upon the deck. "Will she live through it?" he screamed.

"If she isn't driven ashore," cried Bellamy with perfect indifference. "Come nearer; we can't make ourselves heard in this infernal noise."

It did not occur to him to move nearer to Lomax; perhaps he took pride in standing in the middle of the cabin, under the lamp now madly swaying in its gimbals, with the water still dripping from his oilskins into a pool on the floor. Lomax staggered towards him, clinging on to the edge of the bunk. It crossed his mind that this was a strange occasion to choose for conversation, but his standard of strangeness being now somewhat high he did not pause for long to consider that.

"I want to have a talk with you," said Bellamy again.

An enormous shock of water struck the ship overhead, and for a moment she quivered through all her timbers,—a moment of stillness almost, while she ceased to roll, and nothing but that shudder ran through her. "Stood that well," said Bellamy, listening. Then she plunged; plunged as though never to rise any more, falling down as though a trap in the waters had opened to receive her; but she came up, lifted as rapidly as she had fallen, with a tremendous list over on to her side; righted herself, and took again to her rolling. The mate appeared in the doorway.

"Dinghy's gone, sir."

The man poured with water; in his black oilskins, his black

sou'wester, he was a part of the black, wet night made tangible. Bellamy turned to Lomax. "So we're isolated. Not that a boat could have lived in a sea like this."

"What are you really thinking of?" cried Lomax. "Not of the dinghy, or the sea, but something you've had in your mind all these weeks. And why tell it to me? You don't know me," but he remembered that he did not know Miss Whitaker, yet he had married her.

"Know you! Know you!" said Bellamy impatiently. "What's knowing, at best? I want you to do me a favour. I want a promise from you. I know you enough to know you won't refuse it."

"Why do you wear those glasses here?" cried Bellamy, staring at his guest.

Lomax, contriving to seat himself on the edge of the bunk, and holding on to the rod, shouted back, "If I took them off I might refuse any promise."

"I like you," said Bellamy. "I want you to come to me any day I should send for you—in England."

"So we are going back to England, are we?" said Lomax. He remembered their speculations about Bellamy. And so accustomed had he grown to the close limitation of the yacht and their four selves inhabiting it, that the prospect of disintegration was not only unconvincing, but positively distasteful. "We had," he said, "an idea that you wouldn't allow us to go back," but he wondered as he said it why men should take pleasure in bringing pain upon one another.

"Was I so sinister a figure?" said Bellamy. He took off his helmet, shining from the wet, and the lamp over his head gleamed upon his thick white hair and carved the shadows of weariness on his face, shadows that moved and shifted with the swinging of the lamp. "I was inconsiderate, doubtless,—exasperating,—wouldn't make plans,—I owe you all an apology. I am an egoist, you see, Lomax. I was thinking of myself. There were certain things I wanted to allow myself the luxury of forgetting."

It was intolerable that Bellamy should heap this blame upon himself.

"You teased us," muttered Lomax in shamed justification.

"Yes, I teased you," said Bellamy. "I apologise again, I disturbed your comfort. But knowing myself to be a dying man, I indulged myself in that mischief. I had moods, I confess, when the sight of your comfort and your security irritated me even into the desire to drown you all. It's bad thinking, of a very elementary sort, and the foundation of most cynicism. I accept your rebuke."

"Damn you," said Lomax, twisting his hands.

"Nevertheless," Bellamy continued, "I shan't scruple to ask of you the favour I was going to ask. I am a coward, Lomax. I am afraid of pain. I am afraid of disease,—of long, slow, disgusting disease—you understand me? And I have long been looking for some one who, when the moment came, would put me out of it."

"You can count on me," said Lomax. At the same time he could not help hoping that the moment had not come there and then. Procastination and a carefully chosen pair of spectacles would make him a very giant of decision.

Lomax went up on deck; he wanted a storm outside his head as well as a storm within it. The rain had ceased, and the tall spars swayed across a cloudy sky, rent between the clouds to show the moon. The sea was very rough and beautiful beneath the moon. It was good to see the storm at last, to see as well as to feel. Stars appeared, among the rack of the clouds, and vaguely astronomical phrases came into Lomax's mind: Nebulae, Inter-planetary space, Asteroids, Eighty thousand miles a second; he supposed that there were men to whom trillions were a workable reality, just as there were men who could diagnose Bellamy's disease and give him his sentence of death for the sum of two guineas. Two guineas was a contemptible sum to Bellamy, who was so rich a man. To Artivale, what did two guineas mean? A new retort? A supply of chemical? And to Lomax himself,—a new pair of glasses? Tossed on Illyrian billows, he saw a lunar rainbow standing suddenly upon the waves, amazingly coloured in the night of black and silver. Life jumbled madly in his brain. There was Marion, too, lost to him from the moment he had stepped out of that system in which existence was simply a thing to be got through as inconspicuously as possible; and leaning against the deck-house for support he came nearer to tears than he had ever been in his life.

Of course it was to be expected that the death of so wealthy a man as Bellamy should create a certain sensation. There were headlines in the papers, and Arthur Lomax, who had dined with him that evening and had been the last person to see him alive, spent tiresome days evading reports. Veronal it was; no question or doubt about that; the tumbler containing the dregs of poison and the dregs of whisky and soda was found quite frankly standing on the table beside him. Lomax's evidence at the inquest threw no light on the suicide; no, Mr. Bellamy had not appeared depressed; yes, Mr. Bellamy had mixed a whisky and soda and drunk it off in his, Lomax's, presence. He had not seen Mr. Bellamy add anything to the contents of the tumbler. He was unable to say whether Mr. Bellamy had mixed a second whisky and soda after he, Lomax, had left the house. What time had he left? Late; about one in the morning. They had sat up talking. No, he had not known Mr. Bellamy very long, but they had been for a yachting cruise together, lasting some weeks. He would not say that they had become intimate. He knew nothing of Mr. Bellamy's private affairs. He had been very much shocked to read of the death next morning in the papers. Thank you, Mr. Lomax, that will do.

Bellamy was buried, and Lomax, Artivale, and Miss Whitaker attended the funeral, drawn together again into their little group of four,—if you counted Bellamy, invisible, but terribly present, in his coffin. To be buried in the rain is dreary, but to be buried on a morning of gay sunshine is more ironical. Fortunately for Lomax, he was able to obscure the sunshine by the use of his black glasses; and heaven knows he needed them. He was either indifferent or oblivious to the remarkable appearance he offered, in a top-hat, a black coat, and black spectacles. "Weak eyes," noted the reporters. In fact he cared nothing for externals now, especially with the memory of his last meeting with Bellamy strong upon him. On seeing Miss Whitaker he roused himself a little, just enough to look at her with a wondering curiosity; he had forgotten her existence lately, except for the dim but constant knowledge that something stood blocked between him and Marion Vane, a something that wore neither name nor features, and whose materialisation he recognised, briefly puzzled by her importance, as Miss Whitaker. Important yet not important, for, in the muffled world which was his refuge, nothing mattered; events happened, but his mind registered nothing. Marion Vane herself was but a figure coming to him with out-stretched hands, a figure so long desired, wearing that very gesture seemingly so impossible; and, in that gesture finally made, so instantly repudiated. His whole relationship with Marion Vane seemed now condensed into that moment of repudiation. "I am the resurrection and the life," saith the Lord, but the clods thumped down with very convincing finality into Bellamy's grave. Miss Whitaker stood near him, in black, very fragile; yes, she too had her pathos. Whether she had or had not trapped him with a lie . . . well, the lie, and the necessity for the lie, were of a deeper pathos than any truth she might have chosen to exploit. It is less pathetic to have a seducer in Ecuador than to have no seducer anywhere. But she might, thought Lomax, at least have acted up to her own invention. She might, knowing that she was going to meet him at the funeral, at least have thrust a cushion up under her skirt. A coarse man, Lomax. But perhaps she would have thought that irreverent at a funeral. There was no telling what queer superstitions people had; half the time, they did not know themselves, until a test found them out. Perhaps Miss Whitaker had boggled at that. Give her the benefit of the doubt; oh, surely better to credit her with a scruple than with lack of imagination! "I am become the first-fruits of them that sleep"— what did it all mean, anyway? Bellamy and the storm; why should the storm have given Bellamy courage? brought, so to speak, his hitherto only speculative courage to a head? Where was the relationship? What bearing had the extrinsic world upon the intrinsic? Why should the contemplation of life through coloured glasses make that life the easier to ruin? Why should reality recede? What *was* reality? Marion with her hands outstretched; so sure of him. Better to have helped Bellamy; better to have helped Miss Whitaker. Even though Miss Whitaker's need of help was, perhaps, fictitious? Yes, even so. The loss was hers, not his. Her falsity could not impair his quixotism; that was a wild, irrational thing, separate, untouched, independent. It flamed out of his life,—for all the unreality of Miss Whitaker, that actual Miss Whitaker who subscribed to the census paper, paid rates and taxes, and had an existence in the eyes of the law,—it flamed as a few things flamed: his two meetings with Bellamy, his repudiation of Marion Vane. There were just a few gashes of life, bitten in; that was all one could hope for. Was it worth living seventy, eighty years, to accumulate half-a-dozen scars? Half-a-dozen ineradicable pictures, scattered over the monotony of seventy, eighty pages. He had known, when he married Miss Whitaker, that he repudiated Marion Vane; to repudiate her when she came with outstretched hands was but the projection of the half-hour in the Cairo registry office. But it was that that he remembered, and her hurt incredulous eyes; as it was Bellamy's cry that he remembered; always the tangible thing,—such was the weakness of the human, fleshly system. Now Bellamy would rot and be eaten, "Earth to earth, dust to dust"; his sickly body corrupting within the senseless coffin; and by that Lomax would be haunted, rather than by his spiritual tragedy; the tangible again, in the worms crawling in and out of a brain its master had preferred to still into eternal nescience. How long did it take for the buried flesh to become a skeleton? So long, and no less, would Lomax be haunted by the rotting corpse of Bellamy, as he would not have been haunted by the man dragging out a living death. Illogical, all of it; based neither upon truth nor upon reason, but always upon instinct, which reason dismissed as fallacious. Lomax opened his eyes, which he had closed; saw the world darkened, though he knew the sun still shone; and regretted nothing.

He had never before seen Miss Whitaker's house. It was small, and extremely conventional. He sat drinking her tea, and telling himself over and over again that she was his wife. There were letters on her writing-table, and he caught himself looking for the foreign stamp; but he could see nothing but bills. He suspected her correspondence of containing nothing more intimate. Yet here she was, a woman secretly married; that, at any rate, was true, whatever else might be false. He wondered whether she hinted it to her acquaintances, and whether they disbelieved her.

"Why did you laugh?" said Miss Whitaker.

They resumed their conversation. It was feverishly impersonal, yet they both thought it must end by crashing into the shrine of intimacy. But as though their lives depended upon it they juggled with superficiality. Lomax devoted only half his attention to their talk, which indeed was of a nature so contemptibly futile as to deserve no more; the rest of his attention wandered about the room, inquiring into the sudden vividness of Miss Whitaker's possessions: her initials on a paper-cutter, E. A. W.; the photograph of a woman, unknown to him, on the mantelpiece; a little stone Buddha; a seal in the pen-tray. Lomax saw them all through his darkened veil. This was her present,—this small, conventional room; here she opened her morning paper, smoked her after-breakfast cigarette; here she returned in the evening, removed her hat, sat down to a book, poked the fire. But her past stretched away behind her, a blank to Lomax. No doubt she had done sums, worn a pig-tail, cried, and had a mother. So far, conjectures were safe. But her emotional interludes? All locked up? or hadn't there been any? What, to her, was the half-hour in the Cairo registry office? Did it bulk, to her, as Bellamy and Marion Vane bulked to him? One could never feel the shape of another person's mind; never justly apprehend its population. And he was not at all anxious to plumb the possibly abysmal pathos of Miss Whitaker; he didn't want those friends of hers, those strong manly men, to evaporate beneath the crudity of his search. He didn't want to be faced with the true desolation of the little room.

The rumours about Bellamy's death became common property only a few weeks later. They apparently had their origin in Bellamy's will, by which the fortune went to Lomax, turning him from a poor man into a rich one, to his embarrassed astonishment. He wondered vaguely whether the rumours had been set afoot by Miss Whitaker, but came to the conclusion that fact or what she believed to be fact had less allurement for her than frank fiction. Ergo, he said, her seducer in Ecuador interests her more than her secret husband in London. And he reasoned well.

Bellamy's body was exhumed. No one understood why, since the administration of veronal had never been disputed. It was exhumed secretly, at night, by the light of a lantern, and carried into an empty cottage next to the graveyard. The papers next day gave these details. Lomax read them with a nauseous horror. Bellamy, who had abjured life so that his tormented body might be at peace! And now, surrounded by constables, officers of the Law, on a rainy night, lit by the gleams of a hurricane lantern, what remained of his flesh had been smuggled into a derelict cottage and investigated by the scalpel of the anatomist. Truly the grave was neither fine nor private.

Then the newspaper accounts ceased; Bellamy was reburied; and the world went on as usual.

A friendship flared up—surely the queerest in London,—between Lomax and Miss Whitaker. They met quite often. They dined together; they went to theatres. One afternoon they chartered a taxi and did a London round: they went to Sir John Soane's Museum, to Mme. Tussaud's, and the Zoo. Side by side, they looked at Mme. Tussaud's own modelling of Marie Antoinette's severed head fresh from the basket; they listened to somebody's cook beside them, reading from her catalogue: "Mary Antonette, gelatined in 1792; Lewis sixteen,—why, he was gelatined too"; they held their noses in the Small Cats' House, appreciated the Coati, who can turn his long snout up or down, to left or right, without moving his head, and contemplated at length the Magnificent Bird of Paradise, who hopped incessantly, and the Frogmouth, who, of all creation, has in the supremest degree the quality of immobility and identification with his bough. Lomax found Miss Whitaker quite companionable on these occasions. If she told him how often she had observed the Magnificent Bird and the Frogmouth in their native haunts, he liked her none the less for that; a piquancy was added to her otherwise drab little personality, for he was convinced that she had never stirred out of England save in Bellamy's yacht. And certainly there had been neither Magnificent Bird nor Frogmouth in Illyria.

How romantic were the journeys of Miss Whitaker! How picturesque her travelling companions!

It must not be thought, however, that she incessantly talked about herself, for the very reverse was true; the allusions which she let fall were few, but although few they were always most startling.

Her company was usually, if not immediately, available. That was a great advantage to Lomax, who soon found that he could depend upon her almost at a moment's notice. Sometimes, indeed, a little obstacle came back to him over the telephone: "Lunch to-day? oh dear, I am so sorry I can't; I promised Roger that I would lunch with him", or else, "I promised Carmen that I would motor down to Kew." Lomax would express his regret. And Miss Whitaker, "But wait a moment, if you will ring off now I will try to get through to him (or her), and see if I can't put it off." And twenty minutes later Lomax's telephone bell would ring, and Miss Whitaker would tell him how angry Roger (or Carmen) had been, declaring that she was really too insufferable, and that he (or she) would have nothing more to do with her.

Miss Whitaker, indeed, was part of the fantasy of Lomax's life. He took a great interest in Roger and Carmen, and was never tired of their doings or their tempers. He sometimes arrived at Miss Whitaker's house to find a used tea-cup on the tray, which was pointed out to him as evidence of their recent departure. He sympathised over a bruise inflicted by the jealousy of Roger. On the whole, he preferred Carmen, for he liked women to have pretty hands, and Carmen's were small, southern, and dimpled; in fact, he came very near to being in love with Carmen. He beheld them, of course, as he now beheld Miss Whitaker, as he beheld everything, through the miraculous veil of his spectacles; crudity was tempered, criticism in abeyance; only compassion remained, and a vast indifference. All sense of reality had finally left him on the day that he repudiated Marion Vane; he scarcely suffered now, and even the nightmare which was beginning to hem him in held no personal significance; he was withdrawn. He heard the rumours about Bellamy's death, as though they concerned another man. He was quite sure that he regretted nothing he had done.

He was staring at the card he held in his hand: Mr. Robert Whitaker.

So Robert existed. Robert who had scoured Russia to avenge a woman. He was disappointed in Miss Whitaker. Since Robert existed, what need had she to mention him? An imaginary brother might tickle the fancy; a real brother was merely commonplace. With a sigh he gave orders for the admission of Robert. He awaited him, reflecting that the mortification of discovering that which one believed true to be untrue is as nothing compared to the mortification of discovering that which one believed untrue to be true. All art, said Lomax, is a lie; but that lie contains more truth than the truth. But here was Robert.

He was large and angry; lamentably like his sister's presentment of him. Lomax began to believe both in his Persian oil-field and in his exaggerated sense of honour. And when he heard Robert's business, he could no longer cherish any doubts as to Miss Whitaker's veracity. Here was Robert, large as life, and unmistakably out for revenge.

Lomax sat smiling, examining his finger-nails, and assenting to everything. Yes, he had been secretly married to Robert's sister in Cairo. Yes, it was quite possible, if Robert liked to believe it, that he was a bigamist. A seducer of young women. At that Lomax frankly laughed. Robert did not at all like the note in his laughter; mocking? satirical? He did not like it at all. Did Mr. Lomax at least realise that he would have Miss Whitaker's family to reckon with? He, Robert, had heard things lately about Mr. Lomax which he would not specify at present, but which would be investigated, with possibly very unpleasant results for Mr. Lomax. They were things which were making Miss Whitaker's family most uneasy. He did not pretend to know what Lomax's little game had been, but he had come to-day to warn him that he had better lie low and be up to no tricks. Lomax was greatly amused to find himself regarded as an adventurer. He put on a bland manner towards Robert which naturally strengthened Robert's conviction. And his last remark persuaded Robert that he was not only dangerous, but eccentric.

"By the way," he said, stopping Robert at the door, "would you mind telling me whether you have ever been in Russia? And did you catch your man?"

Robert stared angrily, and said, "Yes, to both questions."

"Ah, pity, pity!" said Lomax regretfully, shaking his head. There was another illusion gone.

He was almost tempted to wonder whether he ought not to believe again, as he had believed originally, in the seducer in Ecuador.

When he next saw Miss Whitaker he made no allusion to Robert's visit; neither did she, though she must have known of it. She had received an anonymous letter threatening abduction, and was full of that; she showed it to Lomax, who considered it with suitable gravity. He found Miss Whitaker's adventures most precious to him in his state of life and of mind. He clung on to them, for he knew that his own danger was becoming urgent. He had heard the phrase, "living on a volcano", but until now it had had as little meaning as it has for the rest of us. But now he knew well enough the expectation of being blown, at any moment, sky-high.

With these thoughts in his head, Lomax decided that he must see Artivale before it was too late. Before it was too late. Before, that is to say, he had been deprived of the liberty of action; that was the first step, that deprivation, to be followed by the second step: deprived of speech, gesture, thought,—deprived of life itself. Before he was reduced, first to a prisoner, and then to a limp body lifted from under the gallows by the hands of men.

He must see Artivale.

Artivale lived in Paris. Lomax travelled to Paris, surprised, almost, to find his passport unchallenged and himself unchecked as he climbed into a train or crossed the gangway of a boat. Again and again surprise returned to him, whether he ordered a cup of tea in his Pullman or sat in his corner of the French compartment looking at *La Vie Parisienne* like any ordinary man. He was going to Paris. He had bought his ticket, and the clerk in the booking-office had handed it to him without comment. That meant freedom,—being a free man. The privileges of freedom. He looked at his fellow-travellers and wondered whether they knew how free they were. How free to come and go, and how quickly their freedom might be snatched from them. He wondered what they would say if they knew that a condemned man travelled with them. Time was the important thing; whether he had time enough to do what he had to do before the hand fell upon him. "But", thought Lomax, laughing to himself, "they are all condemned, only they forget about it; they know it, but they forget." And as he looked at them through his spectacles,—the black ones,—moving as though they had eternity before them in a world dim, unreal, and subdued, they seemed to him in their preoccupation and their forgetfulness extremely pitiful.

Under the great girders of the Gare du Nord they scurried, tiny figures galvanised suddenly into shouting and haste. But it was not the recollection of their ultimate condemnation that made them hurry; it was the returning urgency of their own affairs after the passivity of the journey. After all, the train is going as fast as it can, and the most impatient traveller can do no more than allow himself to be carried. But on arrival it is different. Porters may be speeded up by abuse, other travellers may be shoved out of the way, one may capture the first taxi in the rank rather than the last. All these things are of great importance. Perversely, Lomax, as soon as he had descended from the train, began to dawdle. The station, that great cavern full of shadows, swallowing up the gleaming tracks, stopping the monstrous trains as with a wall of finality; those tiny figures so senselessly hurrying; those loads of humanity discharged out of trains from unknown origins towards unknown destinations; all this appeared to him as the work of some crazy etcher, building up a system of lit or darkened masses, here a column curving into relief, there a cavernous exit yawning to engulf, here groins and iron arches soaring to a very heaven of night, there metallic perspectives diminishing towards a promise of day; and everywhere the tiny figures streaming beneath the architectural nightmare, microscopic bodies of men with faces undistinguishable, flying as for their lives along passage-ways between eddies of smoke in a fantastic temple of din and murk and machinery. Moreover, he was wearing, it must be remembered, the black glasses. That which was sombre enough to other eyes, to him was sinister as the pit. He knew the mood which the black glasses induced; yet he had deliberately come away with no other pair in his pocket. The fear which troubled him most was the thought that in his imprisonment his glasses might be taken from him—he had dim recollections, survivals from a life in which the possibility of imprisonment played no part, that condemned criminals must be deprived of all instruments of suicide. And the black glasses, of them all, best suited his natural humour. Therefore he had indulged himself, on perhaps his last opportunity, by bringing no alternative pair. Since he had lost everything in life, he would riot in the luxury of beholding life through an extravagance of darkness.

A dragon pursued him, clanging a bell; mechanically he moved aside, and the electric luggage-trucks passed him, writhing into the customs-house at the end of the station. Artivale lived in the Quartier Latin; it was necessary to get there before the hand fell on his shoulder. Paris taxi-drivers were mad, surely, and their taxis on the verge of disintegration; chasing enormous trams, charged by demoniac lorries, hooting incessantly and incessantly hooted at, Lomax in his wheeled scrap-iron rattled across a Paris darkened into the menace of an imminent cataclysm. A heaven of lead hung over the ghastly streets. All condemned, thought Lomax, as he racketed through the procession of life that was so gaily unconscious of the night in which it moved.

He arrived at Artivale's house.

Artivale himself opened the door.

"Good God!" he said on seeing Lomax, "what . . . But come

in.—You're ill," he continued, when he had got Lomax inside the door.

"No," said Lomax, oblivious of the startling appearance he presented, with haggard cheeks behind the absurd spectacles; "only, I had to see you,—in a hurry."

"In a hurry?" said Artivale, accustomed to think of Lomax as a man without engagements, occupations, or urgency.

"You see," said Lomax, "I murdered Bellamy and I may be arrested at any moment."

"Of course that does explain your hurry," said Artivale, "but would you mind coming down to the kitchen, where I want to keep my eye on some larvae? We can talk there. My servants don't understand English."

Lomax followed him downstairs to the basement, where in a vaulted kitchen enormous blue butterflies circled in the air and a stout negress stoked the oven. The room was dark and excessively hot. "We're in the tropics," said Lomax, looking at the butterflies.

Artivale apologised for the atmosphere. "I have to keep it hot for the sake of the larvae," he explained, "and I had to import the black women because no French servant would stand the heat. These are the larvae," and he showed Lomax various colourless smudges lying on the tables and the dresser. "Now tell me about Bellamy."

The negress beamed upon them benevolently, showing her teeth. A negro girl came from an inner room, carrying a pile of plates. A butterfly of extraordinary brilliancy quivered for a moment on the kitchen clock, and swept away, up into the shadows of the roof, fanning Lomax with its wings in passing.

"The murder was nothing," said Lomax; "he asked me to do it. He was ill, you see,—mortally,—and he was afraid of pain. That's all very simple. He left me his fortune, though."

"Yes," said Artivale, "I read his will in the paper."

"I am leaving that to you," said Lomax.

"To me,—but, my dear fellow, you're not going to die."

"Oh yes," said Lomax, "I shall be hung, of course. Besides, we are all condemned, you know."

"Ultimately, yes," replied Artivale, "but not imminently."

"That's why people forget about it," said Lomax, gazing at him very intently.

Artivale began to wonder whether Lomax suffered from delusions.

"Could you take off those spectacles?" he asked.

"No," said Lomax. "I should go mad if I did. You have no idea how beautiful your butterflies are, seen through them,—the blue through a veil of black. But to go back to the fortune. I ought, perhaps, to leave it to Miss Whitaker, but she has enough of her own already."

"Why to Miss Whitaker?" asked Artivale.

"I married her in Cairo," replied Lomax; "I forgot to tell you that. It is so difficult to remember all these things."

"Are you telling me that you and Miss Whitaker were married all that time on the yacht?"

"Exactly. She was going to have a child, you know,—by another man."

"I see," said Artivale.

"But of course all these things that I am telling you are private."

"Oh, quite," said Artivale. "Miss Whitaker was going to have a child, so you married her; Bellamy had a mortal illness, so you murdered him. Private and confidential. I quite understand."

"I hope you will have no scruples about accepting the fortune," said Lomax anxiously. "I am leaving it to you, really, as I should leave it to a scientific institute,—because I believe you will use it to the good of humanity. But if you make any difficulties I shall alter my will and leave it to the Royal Society."

"Tell me, Lomax," said Artivale, "do you care a fig for humanity?"

"There is nothing else to care about," said Lomax.

"Of course I accept your offer,—though not for myself," said Artivale.

"That's all right then," said Lomax, and he rose to go.

"Stay a moment," said Artivale. "Naturally, you got Bellamy to sign a paper stating that you were about to murder him at his own request?"

"No," said Lomax; "it did cross my mind, but it seemed indelicate, somehow,—egotistic, you know, at a moment like that, to mention such a thing,—and as he didn't suggest it I thought I wouldn't bother him. After all, he was paying me a great compliment,—a very great compliment."

"Oh, undoubtedly!" said Artivale, "but I think, if you will forgive my saying so, that your delicacy outran your prudence. Any evidence that I can give . . ."

"But you have only my word, and that isn't evidence," replied Lomax, smiling.

At that moment a bell pealed through the house upstairs.

"That will be for me," said Lomax; "how lucky that I had time to say what I wanted to say."

"Oh, you *are* lucky, aren't you?" cried Artivale wildly; "a lucky, lucky dog. Your luck's inconceivable. Lomax,—look here,—Lomax,—you must get out of this house. The back door . . ."

The bell rang again.

"It's only a question of sooner or later," said Lomax gently; "for everybody, you know; not only for me. If they let me keep the spectacles I don't mind. With them, I don't see things as they are. Or perhaps I do. It doesn't make much difference which. If you won't go up and open that door, I shall go and open it myself."

They took Lomax away in a cab. He was not allowed to keep his spectacles. Artivale came downstairs again to the kitchen, and watched a peacock butterfly of humming-bird proportions crawl free of its cocoon and spread its wings in flight.

It was only during the course of his trial that Lomax discovered how pitiable a weapon was truth. A law-court is a place of many contradictions; pitch-pine walls and rows of benches give it the appearance of a school treat, white wigs and scarlet and phraseology erect it into a seeming monument to all civilisation, but of the helplessness of the victim there is at least no doubt at all. His bewilderment is the one certain factor. Lomax in the days when he might meet fact with fantasy had been a contented man; now, when he tried to meet with fact the fantastical world which so suddenly and so utterly swamped him, was a man confounded, a man floundering for a foothold. He had lost his spectacles. He had lost his attitude towards life. He had lost Miss Whitaker, or at any rate had exchanged her for a Miss Whitaker new and formidable, a Miss Whitaker who, astonishingly and catastrophically, spoke a portion of the truth. If earth had turned to heaven and heaven to earth a greater chaos could not have resulted in his mind.

The public see me in the dock; they do not see me in my cell. Let me look at the walls; they are white, not clouded into a nameless colour, as once they would have been. Uncompromisingly white.

How ugly, how bare! But I must remember: this is a prison cell. I have no means of turning it into anything else. I am a prisoner on trial for my life. That's fact. A plain man, suffering the consequences for the actions of a creature enchanted, now disappeared. The white walls are fact. Geometry is a fact,—or so they say,—but didn't some one suggest that in another planetary system the laws of geometry might be reversed? This cell is geometrical; square floor, square ceiling, square walls, square window intersected by bars. Geometrical shadows, Euclidean angles. White light. Did I, or did I not, do this, that, and the other? I did, but . . . No buts. Facts are facts. Yes or no. Geometrical questions require geometrical answers. If A be equal to B, then C . . . But either I am mad, or they are mad, or the King's English no longer means what it used to mean.

In the dock again. Amazing statements, in substance true, in essence madly false. He must neither interrupt nor attempt to justify. All these events, which dance round him pointing crooked fingers, disfiguring their aspects into such caricatures, all these events came about so naturally, so inevitably. He knows that, as a lesson learnt, though the enchantment is gone from him. If he might speak, even, what should he relate of that experience? If he might speak! But when he speaks he damns himself. His counsel speaks for him, well-primed, so far as his client's idea of honour has been allowed to prime him; but Lomax knows all the time that his life is of no real consequence to his counsel, except in so far as success provides advertisement; he knows that after the trial is over, one way or the other, his counsel will meet the opposing counsel in the lobby and stop to joke with him, "Got the better of you that time", or, "Well, you were too much for me".

Meanwhile his counsel has been eloquent, in an academic way. Lomax has nothing to complain of. The opening speech for the defence. A simple defence: murder at the victim's request; a man threatened by a mortal disease. An act of friendship; an exaggerated act of friendship, it may be said; but shall it be called the less noble for that? But Lomax sees it coldly; he judges dispassionately, as though the story were not his own. Here stands this man; the jury will hear him tell how, out of compassion for a man he barely knew, he exposed himself to the utmost risk; even the precautions of common prudence were neglected by him in the urgency and delicacy of the circumstances. Another man would have refused this friendly office; or, accepting it, would have ensured his personal safety by a written assurance; or, thirdly, would have hurried from the house before the death had taken place. Not so the prisoner. Prisoner had remained for two hours with the dead body of his friend in the room, dealing with his private papers according to instructions previously received. (Here the prisoner was observed to show some signs of emotion.) Again, the prisoner might have pleaded not guilty; but, regretting his inaccuracies at the time of the inquest, had refused to do so. He was determined to tell the whole truth and to throw himself upon the mercy of the jury.

Lomax realised fully the impossible task his obstinacy had imposed upon his unfortunate counsel.

He realised too, however, that the difficulties improved the game, from the point of view of his counsel. How great would his triumph be, supposing . . .! And, after all, it was nothing but a game.

"A hopeless fellow," said counsel to his wife that night, over his port. "I never had to deal with such a case,—never. Of course, if I can get him off, I'm made," and he fell to ruminating, and his wife, who was in love with him, knew better than to interrupt.

How strange a colour were faces in the mass! A face examined separately and in detail was pink, porous, distinctive with mouth and eyebrows, but taken collectively they were of a uniform buff, and wore but one expression, of imbecile curiosity. Upturned, vacuous curiosity. Lomax had a prolonged opportunity for looking down upon such a mass. Here and there he picked out a face he knew,—Artivale, Robert Whitaker, the captain of the *Nereid*,—and wondered vaguely what strands had drawn them all together at that place. Only by an effort of concentration could he connect them with himself. The voice went on, telling the truth on his behalf. The jury leaned forward to stare at him. The judge, with a long face and dewlaps like a blood-hound, up under his canopy, drew pictures on his blotting-paper. Outside in the streets, sensational posters flowered against the railings with the noonday editions. The Coati in the Zoo waggled his snout; at Mme. Tussaud's the waxen murderers stood accumulating dust in the original dock of the Old Bailey; the *Nereid*, stripped of her wings, swayed a forlorn hulk in the mud at Brightlingsea.

The prosecution was thick with argument. It bore down upon Lomax like a fog through which he could not find his way. He heard his piteous motives scouted; he heard the exquisite ridicule: he saw a smile of derision flicker across the jury. And he sympathised. He quite saw that he could not expect to be believed. If only Bellamy had not left him that fortune, he might have stood a chance. But he would not be so ungenerous as to criticise Bellamy.

That was the first day of the prosecution. Lomax at night in his cell was almost happy: he was glad to endure this for Bellamy's sake. He had loved Bellamy. He was glad to know at last how much he had loved Bellamy. And his privilege had been to spare Bellamy years of intolerable life. He never stopped to argue that Bellamy might just as well have performed the function for himself; for Bellamy was a coward,—had said so once and for all, and Lomax had accepted it. Lomax did not sleep much that night, but a sort of exultation kept him going: he had saved Bellamy, Artivale would have the money, and it was still just possible that to Miss Whitaker he had rendered a service. Not much of a service, certainly, to provide her with a convicted murderer upon whom to father her child; but, between himself and his own conscience, he knew that his intentions had been honourable. His brain was perfectly clear that night. He knew that he must hold on to those three things, and he would go compensated to the scaffold.

On the second day two of his three things were taken from him.

The first was the harder to bear. Post-mortem had revealed no mortal disease in the exhumed body. Lomax, lack-lustre in the dock, stirred to brief interest: so Bellamy, too, had been of the same company? But what Bellamy had really believed would now never be known.

The second concerned Miss Whitaker. Before she was called, the court was cleared, counsel submitting that the evidence about to be produced was of too delicate and private a character for publication. Ah, thought Lomax, here is a delicacy they can understand! He sat quiet while feet shuffled out of the court, herded away by a bailiff. Then when the doors were closed he heard the now familiar voice: Evelyn Amy Whitaker.

She was in the witness-box. She was very much frightened, but she had been subpoenaed, and Robert had terrorised her. She would not look at Lomax. Was she resident at 40 College Buildings, Kensington? She was. She had known the prisoner since April of the present year. She had met him on Mr. Bellamy's yacht. They had sailed from Southampton to Alexandria and from thence had travelled by train to Cairo. In Cairo she had married the prisoner.

Here Lomax's counsel protested that the evidence was irrelevant.

Counsel for the Crown maintained that the evidence was necessary to throw light upon the prisoner's character, and the objection was overruled.

Examination continued: the marriage took place entirely at the prisoner's suggestion. He had appeared very strange, and insisted upon wearing coloured spectacles even when not in the sun,—but here another protest was raised, and allowed by his lordship. Prisoner had always been very much interested in Mr. Bellamy, and occasionally said he could not understand him; also asked witness and Mr. Artivale their opinion. She had never heard Mr. Bellamy make any reference to his health. She had known Mr. Bellamy and the prisoner to be closeted for long talks in Mr. Bellamy's cabin.

Cross-examined by counsel for the defence: was it not a fact that she had led the prisoner to believe that she was with child by a man then living abroad? and that prisoner's suggestion of marriage was prompted by considerations of chivalry? Certainly not.

Dr. Edward Williams, of Harley Street, gynaecologist, examined: he had attended the witness, and could state upon oath that she was not in the condition described. The lady was, in fact, he might add, a virgin.

Lomax listened to this phantasmagoria of truth and untruth. He could have thanked the doctor for the outstanding and indubitable accuracy of his statement. It shone out like a light in darkness.

His lordship, much irritated: "I cannot have this."

As your lordship pleases.

But the jury looked paternally at Miss Whitaker, thinking that she had had a lucky escape.

And again Lomax sympathised with the scepticism of the jury. Again he saw that he could not expect to be believed. "People don't do such things"; men were not quixotic to that extent. Of course they could not believe. Why, he himself, in his pre-spectacle days, would not have believed. He scarcely believed now. The spectacles were really responsible; but it would only make matters worse to tell the jury about the spectacles. There was no place for such things in a tribunal; and, since all life was a tribunal, there should be no place for such things in life. The evidence for the defence was already sufficiently weak. Lomax had never known the name of the doctor who had given Bellamy his death-sentence, and advertisement had failed to produce him. Artivale, an impassioned witness, had had his story immediately pulled to pieces. Lomax himself was examined. But it all sounded very thin. And now that he was deprived of his spectacles—was become again that ordinary man, that Arthur Lomax getting through existence, with only the information of that fantastic interlude, as though it concerned another man, the information rather than the memory, since it existed now for him in words and not in sensation,—now that he was returned to his pre-spectacle days, he could survey his story with cold hard sense and see that it could bear no relation to a world of fact. It was a mistake, he had always known that it was a mistake, to mix one's manners. And for having permitted himself that luxury, he was about to be hanged. It was perhaps an excessive penalty, but Lomax was not one to complain.

Miss Whitaker came to visit him in prison. She was his wife, however shamefully he had treated her, and had no difficulty in obtaining the necessary permission from compassionate authority. Lomax was pleased to see her. She reminded him of Illyria and the Coati,—though, of course, Illyria and the Coati were things he knew of only by hearsay. But Miss Whitaker herself was a little embarrassed; was almost sorry she had come. Like Lomax, she found reality confusing. "I am afraid you have ruined your life," she said, looking round Lomax's neat cell.

"Not at all," said Lomax politely, "so long as I haven't ruined yours. I am only sorry my counsel should have mentioned that about the child. He got it out of me in an unguarded moment. I am glad to have this opportunity of apologising."

"Yes, poor little thing," said Miss Whitaker. "But as my name hasn't appeared, no harm was done. I was sorry, too, that I had to give evidence against you. Robert insisted,—I always warned you that Robert was very revengeful."

"Quite," said Lomax.

"I ought to tell you," said Miss Whitaker, looking down at her shoes, "that *he* is coming home. He has been among the Indians for the last six months, and it has broken his health. He lands at Southampton,—where we sailed from, do you remember?—just before Christmas."

"I am sorry," said Lomax, "that I shan't have the pleasure of meeting him."

"No," said Miss Whitaker; and then, seeming to lose her head a little, she again said, "No; of course you won't. Perhaps I ought to be going?"

Anyway, Artivale would have the money. Lomax hugged that to his breast. Science would have the money; and science was a fact, surely, incapable of caricature; absolute, as mathematics were absolute. He had had enough of living in a world where truth was falsehood and falsehood truth. He was about to abandon that world, and his only legacy to it should be to an incorruptible province; let him hold that comfort, where all other comforts had turned to so ingenious a mockery.

Shortly after Lomax had been hanged, Bellamy's nearest relations, two maiden ladies who lived at Hampstead and interested them-selves in the conversion of the heathen, entered a plea that Bellamy's will had been composed under the undue influence of Arthur Lomax. The case was easily proved, and it was understood that the bulk of the fortune would be placed by the next-of-kin as conscience money at the disposal of His Majesty's Treasury.

THE END

Vita Sackville-West

THE HEIR
A Love Story

TO BM

FOREWORD

I wrote this story in 1922, or it might be 1921. There can be no indiscretion now in revealing that it was inspired by Groombridge Place, astride the borders of Kent and Sussex.

I had always known Groombridge Place and the two old Misses Sant who lived there. After the death of the last Miss Sant, when the property came up for sale, I went there with a rich and florid South American acquaintance of mine, who thought of buying it, and whose attitude towards it shocked me into writing this story. It shocked me also into inventing my Mr. Chase, a purely imaginary character, heir to a tradition he had never envisaged, which caught him so unexpectedly into its toils.

I had not read my story for twenty-seven years, when Mr. Martin Secker asked me to let him reprint it. Then I re-read it, with that obituary feeling one has towards one's youthful work. Can I let it stand, I wondered? Is it too slight? Is it too mawkishly sentimental? Or is it so sincerely felt that it can still stand on its own legs? Sincerity, as I now know, is not enough; it is not the true touch-stone; it is the delusion which drives many a writer into believing himself a better writer than he is. Yet I came to the conclusion that it reflected a mood I had felt then and have felt with increasing melancholy ever since; so here, for better or worse, it is.

V.S.-W

Sissinghurst 1949

I

Miss Chase lay on her immense red silk four-poster that reached as high as the ceiling. Her face was covered over by a sheet, but as she had a high, aristocratic nose, it raised the sheet into a ridge, ending in a point. Her hands could also be distinguished beneath the sheet, folded across her chest like the hands of an effigy; and her feet, tight together like the feet of an effigy, raised the sheet into two further points at the bottom of the bed. She was eighty-four years old, and she had been dead for twenty-four hours.

The room was darkened into a shadowy twilight. Outside, in a pale, golden sunshine, the birds twittered among the very young green of the trees. A thread of this sunshine, alive with golden dust-motes, sundered the curtain, and struck out, horizontally, across the boards of the floor. One of the two men who were moving with all possible discretion about the room, paused to draw the curtains more completely together.

"Very annoying, this delay about the coffin," said Mr. Nutley. "However, I got off the telegrams to the papers in time, I hope, to get the funeral arrangements altered. It would be very awkward if people from London turned up for the funeral on Thursday instead of Friday—very awkward indeed. Of course, the local people wouldn't turn up; they would know the affair had had to be put off; but London people—they're so *scattered*. And they would be annoyed to find they had given up a whole day to a country funeral that wasn't to take place after all."

"I should think so, indeed," said Mr. Chase, peevishly. "I know the value of time well enough to appreciate that."

"Ah yes," Mr. Nutley replied with sympathy, "you're anxious to be back at Wolverhampton, I know. It's very annoying to have one's work cut into. And if *you* feel like that about it, when the old lady was your aunt, what would comparative strangers from London feel, if they had to waste a day?"

They both looked resentfully at the stiff figure under the sheet on the bed, but Mr. Chase could not help feeling that the solicitor was a little over-inclined to dot his i's in the avoidance of any possible hypocrisy. He reflected, however, that it was, in the long run, preferable to the opposite method of Mr. Farebrother, Nutley's senior partner, who was at times so evasive as to be positively unintelligible.

"Very tidy, everything. H'm—handkerchiefs, gloves, little bags of lavender in every drawer. Yes, just what I should have expected: she was a rare one for having everything spick and span. She'd go for the servants, tapping her stick sharp on the boards, if anything wasn't to her liking; and they all scuttled about as though they'd been wound up after she'd done with them. I don't know what you'll do with the old lady's clothes, Mr. Chase. They wouldn't fetch much, you know, with the exception of the lace. There's fine, real lace here, that ought to be worth something. It's all down in the heirloom book, and it'll have to be unpicked off the clothes. But for the rest say twenty pounds. These silk dresses are made of good stuff, I should say," observed Mr. Nutley, fingering a row of black dresses that hung inside a cupboard, and that as he stirred them moved with the faint rustle of dried leaves; "take my advice, and give some to the housekeeper; that'll be of more value to you in the end than the few pounds you might get for them. Always get the servants on your side, is my axiom. However, it's your affair; you're the sole heir, and there's nobody to interfere." He said this with a sarcastic inflection detected only by himself; a warning note under the ostensible deference of his words as though daring Chase to assert his rights. "And, anyway," he concluded, "we're not likely to find any more papers in here, so we're wasting time now. Shall we go down?"

"Wait a minute, listen: what's that noise out in the garden?"

"Oh, that! One of the peacocks screeching. There are at least fifty of the damned birds. Your aunt wouldn't have one of them killed, not one. They ruin a garden. Your aunt liked the garden, and she liked the peacocks, but she liked the peacocks better than the garden.

Screech, screech—you'll soon do away with them. At least, I should say you *would* do away with them if you were going to live here. I can see you're a man of sense."

Mr. Chase drew Mr. Nutley and his volubility out on to the landing, closing the door behind him. The solicitor ruffled the sheaf of papers he carried in his hand, trying to peep between the sheets that were fastened together by an elastic band.

"Well," he said briskly, "if you're agreeable I think we might go downstairs and find Farebrother and Colonel Stanforth. You see, we are trying to save you all the time we possibly can. What about the old lady? Do you want anyone sent in to sit with her?"

"I really don't know," said Chase, "what's usually done? You know more about these things than I do."

"Oh, as to that, I should think I ought to!" Nutley replied with a little self-satisfied smirk. "Perhaps you won't believe me, but most weeks I'm in a house with a corpse. There are usually relatives, of course, but in this case if you wanted anyone sent in to sit with the old lady, we should have to send a servant. Shall I call Fortune?"

"Perhaps you had better—but I don't know: Fortune is the butler, isn't he? Well, the butler told me all the servants were very busy."

"Then it might be as well not to disturb them? At any rate, the old lady won't run away," said Mr. Nutley jocosely.

"No, perhaps we needn't disturb them." Chase was relieved to escape the necessity of giving an order to a servant.

They went downstairs together.

"Hold on to the banisters, Mr. Chase; these polished stairs are very tricky. Fine old oak; solid steps too; but I prefer a drugget myself. Good gracious, how that peacock startled me! Look at it, sitting on the ledge outside the window. It's pecking at the panes with its beak. Shoo, you great gaudy thing." The solicitor flapped his arms at it, like a skinny crow beating its wings.

They stopped to look at the peacock, which, walking the outside ledge with spread tail, seemed to form part, both in colour and pattern, of the great heraldic window on the landing of the staircase. The sunlight streamed through the colours, and the square of sunlight on the boards was chequered with patches of violet, red and indigo.

"Gaudy?" said Chase. "It's barbaric. Like jewels. Astonishing."

Mr. Nutley glanced at him with a faint contempt. Chase was a sandy, weakly-looking little man, with thin reddish hair, freckles, and washy blue eyes. He wore an old Norfolk jacket and trousers that did not match; Mr. Nutley, in his quick impatient mind, set him aside as reassuringly insignificant.

"Farebrother and Colonel Stanforth are in the library, I believe," Nutley suggested.

"Don't forget to introduce me to Colonel Stanforth," said Chase, dismayed at having to meet yet another stranger. "He was an intimate friend of my aunt's, wasn't he? Is he the only trustee?"

"The other one died and was never replaced. As for Colonel Stanforth being an intimate friend of the old lady, he was indeed; about the only friend she ever had; she frightened everybody else away," said Nutley, opening the library door.

"Ah, Mr. Chase!" Mr. Farebrother exclaimed in a relieved and propitiatory tone.

"We've been through all the drawers," Mr. Nutley said, his briskness redoubled in his partner's presence. "We've got all the necessary papers—they weren't even locked up—so now we can get to business. With any luck Mr. Chase ought to see himself back at Wolverhampton within the week, in spite of the delay over the funeral. I've told Mr. Chase that it isn't strictly correct to open the papers before the funeral is over, but that, having regard to his affairs in Wolverhampton, and in view of the fact that there are no other relatives whose susceptibilities we might offend, we are setting to work at once." He was bending over the table, sorting out the papers as he talked, but now he looked up and saw Chase still standing in embarrassment near the door. "Dear me, I was forgetting. Mr. Chase, you don't know Colonel Stanforth, your trustee, I think? Colonel Stanforth has lived outside the park gates all his life, and I wager he knows every acre of your estate better than you ever will yourself, Mr. Chase."

Mr. Farebrother, a round little rosy man in large spectacles, smiled benignly as Chase and Stanforth shook hands. He liked bringing the heir and the trustee together, but his pleasure was clouded by Nutley's last remark, suggesting as it did that Chase would never have the opportunity of learning his estate; he felt this remark to be in poor taste.

"Oh, come! I hope we shall have Mr. Chase with us for some time," he said pleasantly, "although," he added, recollecting himself, "under such melancholy circumstances." He had never been known to make any more direct allusion to death than that contained in this or similarly consecrated phrases. Mr. Nutley pounced instantly upon the evasion.

"After all, Farebrother, Chase never knew the old lady, remember. The melancholy part of it, to my mind, is the muddle the estate is in. Mortgaged up to the last shilling, and overrun with peacocks. Won't you come and sit at the table. Mr. Chase? Here's a pencil in case you want to make any notes."

Colonel Stanforth came up to the table at the same time. Chase shied away, and went to sit on the window-seat. Mr. Farebrother began a little preamble.

"We sent for you immediately, Mr. Chase; that is to say, Colonel Stanforth, who was on the spot at the moment of the regrettable event, communicated with us and with you simultaneously. We should like to welcome you, with all the sobriety required by the cloud which must hang over this occasion, to the estate which has been in the possession of your family for the past five hundred years. We should like to express our infinite regret at the embarrassments under which the estate will be found to labour. We should like to assure you—I am speaking now for my partner and myself—that our firm has been in no way responsible for the management of the property. Miss Chase, your aunt, whom I immensely revered, was a lady of determined character and charitable impulses. . ."

"You mean, she was an obstinate old sentimentalist," said Mr. Nutley, losing his patience.

Mr. Farebrother looked gently pained.

"Charitable impulses," he repeated, "which she was always loth to modify. Colonel Stanforth will tell you that he has had many a discussion . . ." ("I should just think so," said Colonel Stanforth, "you could argue the hind leg off a donkey, but you couldn't budge Phillida Chase,") "there were questions of undesirable tenants and what not—I confess it saddens me to think of Blackboys so much encumbered. . ."

"Encumbered! My good man, the place will be in the market as soon as I can get it there," said Mr. Nutley, interrupting again, and tapping his pencil on the table.

"It would have been so pleasant," said Mr. Farebrother sighing, "if matters had been in an entirely satisfactory condition, and our duty towards Mr. Chase would have been so joyfully fulfilled. Your family, Mr. Chase, were Lords of the Manor of Blackboys long before any house was built upon this site. The snapping of such a chain of tradition . . ."

"Out of date, out of date, my good man," said Nutley, full of contempt and surprisingly spiteful.

"Let's get on to the will," suggested Stanforth.

Mr. Nutley produced it with alacrity.

"Dear, dear," said Mr. Farebrother, wiping his spectacles. The reading of a will was to him always a painful proceeding. It was indeed an unkind fate which had cast one of his amiable and conciliatory nature into the melancholy regions of the law.

"It's very short," said Nutley, and read it aloud.

After providing for a legacy of five hundred pounds to the butler, John Fortune, in recognition of his long and devoted service, and for a legacy of two hundred and fifty pounds to her friend Edward Stanforth "in anticipation of services to be rendered after my death," the testator devised the Manor of Blackboys and the whole of the Blackboys Estate and all other messuages tenements hereditaments and premises situate in the counties of Kent and Sussex and elsewhere and all other estates and effects whatsoever and wheresoever both real and personal to her nephew Peregrine Chase at present of Wolverhampton.

"Sensible woman—she got a solicitor to draw up her will," said Mr. Nutley as he ended; "no side-tracks, no ambiguities, no bother. Sensible woman. Now we can get to work."

"Ah, dear!" said Mr. Farebrother in wistful reminiscence, "how well I remember the day Miss Chase sent for me to assist her in the making of that will; it was just such a day as this, and after I had been waiting a little while she came into the room, a black lace scarf on her white hair, and her beautiful hands leaning on the top of her stick—she had very beautiful hands, your aunt, Mr. Chase, beautiful cool ivory hands—and I remember she was singularly gracious, singularly gracious; a great lady of the old school, and she was pleased to twit me about my reluctance to admit that some day even *she* . . . ah, well, will-making is a painful matter; but I remember her, gallant as ever. . ."

"That's all rubbish, Farebrother," said Mr. Nutley rudely, as his partner showed signs of meandering indefinitely on; "gracious, indeed! When you know she terrified you nearly out of your life. You always get mawkish like this about people once they're dead."

Mr. Farebrother blinked mildly, and Nutley continued without taking any further notice of him.

"You haven't done so well out of this as John Fortune," he said to Stanforth, "and you'll have a deal more trouble."

"I take it," said Stanforth, getting up and striding about the room "that in the matter of this estate there are a great many liabilities and no assets to speak of, except the estate itself? To start with, there's a twenty-thousand-pound mortgage. What's the income from the farms?"

"A bare two thousand a year."

"So you start the year with a deficit, having paid off your income tax and the interest on the mortgage. Disgusting," said Stanforth. "One thing, at any rate, is clear: the place must go. One could just manage to keep the house, of course, but I don't see how anyone could affort to live in it, having kept it. The land isn't worth over much, but luckily we've got the house and gardens. What figure, Nutley? Thirty thousand? Forty?"

Mr. Nutley whistled.

"You're optimistic. The house isn't so very large, and it's inconvenient, no bathrooms, no electric light, no garage, no central heating. The buyer would have all that on his hands, and the moat ought to be cleaned out too. It's insanitary."

"Still, the house is historical," said Stanforth; "I think we can safely say thirty thousand for the house. It's a perfect specimen of Elizabethan, so I've always been told, and has the Tudor moat and outbuildings into the bargain. Thirty thousand for the house," he noted on a piece of paper.

"I wouldn't care for it myself," said Mr. Nutley, looking round, "low rooms, dark passages, a stinking moat, and a slippery staircase. If that's Tudor, you're welcome to it." His voice had a peculiarly malignant intonation. "Still, it's a gentleman's place, I don't deny, and ought to make an interesting item under the hammer." He passed the tip of his tongue over his lips, a gesture horridly voluptuous in one so sharp and meagre.

"Then we have the furniture and the tapestries and the pictures," Stanforth went on. "I think we might reckon another twenty thousand for them. Americans, you know—or the buyer of the house might care for some of the furniture. The pictures aren't of much value, so I understand, save as of family interest. Twenty thousand. That clears off the mortgage. What about the farms and the land?"

"You could split some of the park up into building lots," said Mr. Nutley.

Mr. Farebrother gave a little exclamation.

"The park—it's a pretty park, Nutley."

"Very pretty, and any builder who chose to run up half a dozen villas would be a sensible chap," Mr. Nutley replied, wilfully misunderstanding him. "I should suggest a site at the top of the hill, where you get the view. What do you think, Colonel Stanforth?"

"I think the buyer of the house should be given the option of buying in the whole of the park, that section being reserved at the price of accommodation land, if he chooses to pay for it."

Mr. Nutley nodded. He approved of Colonel Stanforth as an adequately shrewd business man.

"There remain the farm lands," he said, referring to his papers. "Two thousand acres, roughly; three good farm houses; and a score of cottages. It's a little difficult to price. Say, taking one thing in with another, twenty pounds an acre, including the buildings—a good deal of the land is worth less. Forty thousand. We've disposed now of all the assets. We shall be lucky if we can clear the death-duties and mortgage out of the proceeds of the sale, and let Mr. Chase go with whatever amount the house itself fetches to bring him in a few hundreds a year for the rest of his life."

They stared across at Chase, whose concern with the affair they appeared hitherto to have forgotten. Mr. Farebrother alone kept his eyes bent down, as very meticulously he sharpened the point of his pencil.

"It's an unsatisfactory situation," said Mr. Nutley; "if I were Chase I should resent being dragged away from my ordinary business on such an unprofitable affair. He'll be lucky, as you say, if he clears the actual value of the house for himself after everything is settled up. Now, are we to try for auction or private treaty? Personally I think the house at any rate will go by private treaty. The present tenants will probably buy in their own farms. But the house, if it's reasonably well advertised, ought to attract a number of private buyers. We must have a decent caretaker to show people over the place. I suggest the present butler? He was in Miss Chase's service for thirty years." He looked around for approval; Chase and Stanforth both nodded, though Chase felt so much of an outsider that he wondered whether Nutley would consider him justified in nodding. "Ring the bell, Farebrother, will you? It's just behind you. Look at the bell, gentlemen! What an antiquated arrangement! There's no doubt, the house is terribly inconvenient."

Fortune, the butler, came in, a thin grizzled man in decent black.

"Perhaps you had better give your instructions, Nutley," Chase said from the window-seat as the solicitor glanced at him with conventional hesitation.

"I'm speaking for Mr. Chase, Fortune," said Mr. Nutley. "Your late mistress's will unfortunately isn't very satisfactory, and Blackboys will be in the market before very long. We want you to stay on until then, with such help as you need, and you must tell the other servants they have all a month's notice. By the way, you inherit five hundred pounds under the will, but it'll be some time before you get it."

"Blackboys in the market?" Fortune began.

"Oh, my good man, don't start lamenting again here," exclaimed Mr. Nutley hurriedly; "think of those five hundred pounds—a very nice little sum of which we should all be glad, I'm sure."

"Dear me, dear me," said Mr. Farebrother, much distressed, and he got up and patted Fortune on the shoulder.

Nutley was collecting the papers again into a neat packet, boxing them together on the table as though they had been a pack of cards. He glanced up to say,

"That settled, Fortune? Then we needn't keep you any longer; thanks. Well, Mr. Chase, if there's anything we can do for you to-morrow, you have only to ring me up or Farebrother—oh, I forgot, of course, you aren't on the telephone here."

Chase, who had been thinking to himself that Nutley was a splendid man—really efficient, a first-class man, was suddenly aware that he resented the implied criticism.

"I can go to the post-office if I want to telephone," he said coldly.

Mr. Farebrother noticed the coldness in his tone, and thought regretfully, "Dear me, Nutley has offended him—ignored him completely all the time. I ought to have put that right—very remiss of me."

He said aloud, "If Mr. Chase would prefer not to sleep in the house, I should be very glad to offer him hospitality . . ."

"Afraid of the old lady's ghost, Chase?" said Mr. Nutley with a laugh that concealed a sneer.

They all laughed, with exception of Mr. Farebrother, who was pained.

Chase was tired; he wished they would go; he wanted to be alone.

II

He was alone; they had gone, Stanforth striding off across the park in his rather ostentatious suit of large checks and baggy knicker-bockers, the two solicitors, with their black leather hand-bags, trundling down the avenue in the station cab. They had gone, they and their talk of mortgages, rents, acreage, tenants, possible buyers, building lots, and sales by auction or private treaty! Chase stood on the bridge above the moat, watching their departure. He was still a little confused in his mind, not having had time to turn round and think since Stanforth's telegram had summoned him that morning. Arrived at Blackboys, he had been immediately commandeered by Nutley, had had wishes and opinions put into his mouth, and had found a complete set of intentions ready-made for him to assume as his own. That had all saved him a lot of trouble, undoubtedly; but nevertheless he was glad of a breathing-space; there were things he wanted to think over; ideas he wanted to get used to . . .

He was poor; and hard-working in a cheerless fashion; he managed a branch of a small insurance company in Wolverhampton, and expected nothing further of life. Not very robust, his days in an office left him with little energy after he had conscientiously carried out his business. He lived in lodgings in Wolverhampton, smoking rather too much and eating rather too little. He had always known that some day, when his surviving aunt was dead, he would inherit Blackboys, but Blackboys was only a name to him, and he had gauged that the inheritance would mean for him little but trouble and interruption, and that once the whole affair was wound up he would resume his habitual existence just where he had dropped it.

His occupations and outlook might thus be comprehensively summarized.

He turned to look back at the house. Any man brighter-hearted and more optimistic might have rejoiced in this enforced expedition as a holiday, but Chase was neither optimistic nor bright-hearted. He took life with a dreary and rather petulant seriousness, and, full of resentment against this whole unprofitable errand, was dwelling now upon the probable, the almost certain, inefficiencies of his subordinates in Wolverhampton, because he had in him an old-maidish trait that could not endure the thought of other people interfering with his business or his possessions. He worried, in his small anaemic mind that was too restricted to be contemptuous, and too diffident to be really bad-tempered ... The house looked down at him, grave and mellow. Its façade of old, plum-coloured bricks, the inverted V of the two gables, the rectangles of the windows, and the creamy stucco of the little colonnade that joined the two projecting wings, all reflected unbroken in the green stillness of the moat. It was not a large house; it consisted only of the two wings and the central block, but it was complete and perfect; so perfect, that Chase, who knew and cared nothing about architecture, and whose mind was really absent, worrying, in Wolverhampton, was gradually softened into a comfortable satisfaction. The house was indeed small, sweet, and satisfying. There was no fault to be found with the house. It was lovely in colour and design. It carried off, in its perfect proportions, the grandeur of its manner with an easy dignity. It was quiet, the evening was quiet, the country was quiet; it was part of the evening and the country. The country was almost unknown to Chase, whose life had been spent in towns—factory towns. Here he was on the borders of Kent and Sussex where the nearest town was a village, a jumble of cottages round a green, at his own park-gates. The house seemed to lie at the very heart of peace.

A little wooden gate, moss-grown and slightly dilapidated, cut off the bridge from the gravelled entrance-space; he shut and latched it, and stood on the island that the moat surrounded. Swallows were swooping along the water, for the air was full of insects in the golden haze of the May evening. Faint clouds of haze hung about, blue and gold, deepening the mystery of the park, shrouding the recesses of the garden. The place was veiled. Chase put out his hand as though to push aside a veil . . .

He detected himself in the gesture, and glanced round guiltily to see whether he was observed. But he was alone; even the curtains behind the windows were drawn. He felt a desire to explore the garden, but hesitated, timorous and apologetic. Hitherto in his life he had explored only other people's gardens on the rare days when they were opened to the public; he remembered with what pained incredulity he had watched the public helping itself to the flowers out of the borders, for he could not help being a great respecter of property. He prided himself, of course, on being a Socialist; that was the fashion amongst the young men he occasionally frequented in Wolverhampton; but unlike them he was a Socialist whose sense of veneration was deeper and more instinctive than his socialism. He had thought at the time that he would be very indignant if he were the owner of the garden. Now that he actually was the owner, he hesitated before entering the garden, with a sense of intrusion. Had he caught sight of a servant he would certainly have turned and strolled off in the opposite direction.

The house lay in the hollow at the bottom of a ridge of wooded hills that sheltered it from the north, but the garden was upon the slope of the hill, in design quite simple: a central walk divided the square garden into halves, eased into very flat, shallow steps, and outlined by a low stone coping. A wall surrounded the whole garden. To reach the garden from the house, you crossed a little footbridge over the moat, at the bottom of the central walk. This simplicity, so obvious, yet, like the house, so satisfying, could not possibly have been otherwise ordered; it was married to the lie of the land. It flattered Chase with the delectable suggestion that he, a simple fellow, could have conceived and carried out the scheme as well as had the architect.

He was bound to admit that a simple fellow would not have thought of the peacocks. They were the royal touch that redeemed the gentle friendliness of the house and garden from all danger of complacency. He paused in amazement now at his first real sight of them. All the way up the low wall on either side of the central walk they sat, thirty or forty of them, their long tails sweeping down almost to the ground, the delicate crowns upon their heads erect in a feathery line of perspective, and the blue of their breasts rich above the grey stone coping. Half way up the walk, the coping was broken by two big stone balls, and upon one of these a peacock stood with his tail fully spread behind him, and uttered his discordant cry as though in the triumph and pride of his beauty.

Chase paused. He was too shy even to disturb those regal birds. He imagined the swirl of colour and the screech of indignation that would accompany his advance, and before their arrogance his timidity was abashed. But he stood there for a very long while, looking at them, until the garden became swathed in the shrouds of the blue evening, very dusky and venerable. He did not pass over the moat, but stood on the little bridge, between the house and the garden, while those shrouds of evening settled with the hush of vespers round him, and as he looked he kept saying to himself "Mine? *Mine?*" in a puzzled and deprecatory way.

III

When Fortune showed him his room before dinner he was silent and inclined to scoff. He had been shown the other rooms by Nutley when he first arrived, and had gazed at them, accepting them without surprise, much as he would have gazed at rooms in some show-place or princely palace that he had paid a shilling to visit. The hall, the dining-room, the library, the long gallery—he had looked at them all, and had nodded in reply to the solicitor's comments, but not for a moment had it entered his head to regard the rooms as his own. To be left, however, in this room that resembled all the others, and to be told that it was his bedroom; to realize that he was to sleep inside that brocaded four-poster with the ostrich plumes nodding on the top; to envisage the trivial and vulgar functions of his daily dressing and undressing as taking place within this room that although so small was yet so stately—this was a shock that made him draw in his breath. Left alone, his hand raised to give a tug at his tie, he stared round and emitted a soft whistle. The walls were hung with tapestry, a grey-green landscape of tapestry, the borders formed by two fat twisted columns, looped across with garlands of flowers and fruits, and cherubs with distended cheeks blew zephyrs across this woven Arcady. High-backed Stuart chairs of black and gold . . . Chase wanted to take off his boots, but did not venture to sit down on the tawny cane-work. He moved about gingerly, afraid of spoiling something. Then he remembered that everything was his to spoil if he so chose. Everything waited on his good pleasure; the whole house, all those rooms, the garden; all those unknown farms and acres that Nutley and Stanforth had discussed. The thought produced no exhilaration in him, but, rather, an extreme embarrassment and alarm. He was more than ever dismayed to think that someone, sooner or later, was certain to come to him for orders . . .

He hesitated for an appreciable time before making up his mind to go down to dinner; in fact, even after he had resolutely pushed open his bedroom door, he still wavered upon its threshold. The landing, lit by the yellow flame of a solitary candle stuck into a silver sconce, was full of shadows: and across the great window red velvet curtains had been drawn, and now hung from floor to ceiling. Down the passage, behind one of those mysterious closed doors, lay the old woman dead in her pompous bed. So the house must have drowsed, evening after evening, before Chase ever came near it, with the only difference that from one of those doors had emerged an old lady dressed in black silk, leaning on a stick, an arbitrary old lady, who had slowly descended the polished stairs, carefully placing the rubber ferule of her stick from step to step, and helping herself on the banisters with the other hand, instead of the alien clerk from Wolverhampton, who hesitated to go downstairs to dinner because he feared there would be a servant in the room to wait upon him.

There was. Chase dined miserably, and was relieved only when he was left alone, port and madeira set before him, and the four candles reflected in the shining oak table. A greyhound which had joined him at the foot of the stairs, now sat gravely beside him, and he gave him bits of biscuit as he had not dared to do in the presence of the servant. More at his ease at last, he sat thinking what he would do with the few hundreds a year Nutley predicted for him. Not such an unprofitable business after all, perhaps! He would be able to move from his lodgings in Wolverhampton; perhaps he could take a small villa with a little bit of garden in front. His imagination did not extend beyond Wolverhampton. Perhaps he could keep back one or two pieces of plate from the sale; he would like to have something to remind him of his connexion with Blackboys and with his family. He cautiously picked up a porringer that was the only ornament on the table, and examined it. It gave him a little shock of familiarity to see that the coat-of-arms engraved on it was the same as the coat on his own signet ring, inherited from his father, and the motto was the same too: *Intabescantque relictâ*, and the tiny peregrine falcon as the crest. Absurd to be surprised! He ought to remember that he wasn't a stranger here; he was Chase, no less than the old lady had been

Chase, no less than all the portraits upstairs were Chase. He had already seen that coat-of-arms to-day, in the heraldic window, but without taking in its meaning. It gave him a new sense of confidence now, reassuring him that he wasn't the interloper he felt himself to be.

It was pleasant enough to linger here, with silence and shadows all round the pool of candlelight, that lit the polish of the table, the curves of the silver, and the dark wine in the round-bellied decanters; pleasant to dream of that villa which might now be attainable; but he had better go, or the servant would be coming to clear away.

Rising, he went out into the hall, followed by the dog, who seemed to have adopted him unquestioningly. As Chase didn't know his name, he bent down to read the inscription on the collar, but found only the address: CHASE, BLACKBOYS. That had been the old lady's address, of course, but it would do for him too; he needn't have the collar altered. CHASE, BLACKBOYS. It was simply handed on; no change. It gave him a queer sensation; this coming to Blackboys was certainly a queer experience, interrupting his life. He scarcely knew where he was as yet, or what he was doing; he had to keep reminding himself with an effort.

In the hall he hesitated, uncertain as to which was the door of the library, afraid that if he opened the wrong door he would find himself in the servants' quarters, perhaps even open it on them as they sat at supper. The dog stood in front of one door, wagging his tail and looking up at Chase, so he tried the handle; it was the wrong door, but instead of leading to the servants' quarters it opened straight on to the moonlit garden. The greyhound bounded out and ran about in the moonlight, a wraith of a dog in the ghostly garden. Ghostly ... Chase wandered out, up the walk to the top of the hill, where he turned to look down upon the house, folded black in the hollow, the moonlight gleaming along the moat and winking on a window. Not a breath ruffled that milky stillness; the great cloths of light lay spread out over the grass, the blocks of shadow were profound; above the low-lying park trailed a faint white mist, and in a vaporous sky the moon rode calm and sovereign. Chase felt that on a scene so perfectly set something ought to happen. A pity that it should all be wasted ... How many such nights must have been wasted! The prodigal loveliness of summer nights, lying illusory under the moon, shamelessly soliciting romance! But nothing happened; there was nothing but Chase looking down on the silent house, looking for a long time down on the silent house, and thinking that, on that night so set for a lovers' meeting, no lovers had met.

IV

He was very glad when the funeral was over, and he was rid of all the strange neighbours who had wrung his hand and uttered commiserating phrases. He was also glad that the house should be relieved of the presence of his aunt, for he could tread henceforth unrestrained by the idea that the corpse might rise up and with a pointing finger denounce his few and timorous orders. He stood now on the threshold of the library downstairs, looking at a bowl of coral-coloured tulips whose transparent delicacy detached itself brightly in the sober panelled room. He was grateful to the quietness that slumbered always over the house, abolishing fret as by a calm rebuke.

His recollections of the funeral were, he found to his dismay, principally absurd. Mr. Farebrother had sidled up to him, when he thought Nutley was preoccupied elsewhere, as they returned on foot up the avenue after the ceremony. "A great pity the place should have to go," Mr. Farebrother had said, trotting along beside him, "such a very great pity." Chase had agreed in a perfunctory way. "Perhaps it won't come to that," said Mr. Farebrother with a vague hopefulness. Chase again murmured something in the nature of agreement. "I like to think things will come right until the moment they actually go wrong," Mr. Farebrother said with a smile. "Very sad, too, the death of your aunt," he added. "Yes," said Chase. "Well, well, perhaps it isn't so bad as we think," said Mr. Farebrother, causing Chase to stare at him, thoroughly startled this time by the extent of the rosy old man's optimism.

But he was not now dwelling upon the funeral. To-morrow he must leave Blackboys. No doubt he would find his affairs in Wolverhampton in a terrible way. He said to himself, "Tut-tut," his mind absent, though his eyes were still upon the tulips; but his annoyance over the office in Wolverhampton was largely superficial. Business had a claim on him, certainly; the business of his employers; but his own private business had a claim too, that, moreover, would take up but a month or two out of his life; after that Blackboys would be sold, and would engage no more of his time away from Wolverhampton. Blackboys would pass to other hands, making no further demands upon Peregrine Chase. It would be a queer little incident to look back upon; his few acquaintances in Wolverhampton, with whom he sometimes played billiards of an evening, or joined in a whist drive, would stare, derisive and incredulous, if the story ever leaked out, at the idea of Chase as a landed proprietor. As a squire! As the descendant of twenty generations! Why, no one in Wolverhampton knew so much as his Christian name; he had been careful always to sign his letters with a discreet initial, so that if they thought of it at all they probably thought him Percy. A friend would have nosed it out. There was a safeguard in friendlessness. Chase was a reticent little man, as his solicitors had had occasion to remark. Nutley found this very convenient: Chase, making no comment, left him free to manage everything according to his own ideas. Indeed, Nutley frequently forgot his very existence. It was most convenient.

As for Chase, he wondered sometimes absently which he disliked least: Farebrother with his weak sentimentality, or Nutley, who was so astute, so bent upon getting Blackboys brilliantly into the market, and whose grudging respect for old Miss Chase, beneath his impatience of the tyranny she had imposed upon him, was so readily divined.

Chase stood looking at the bowl of tulips; it seemed to him that he spent his days for ever looking at something, and deriving from it that new, quiet satisfaction. He was revolving in his mind a phrase of Mr. Farebrother's, to the effect that he ought to go the rounds and call upon his tenants. "They'll expect it, you know," Farebrother had said, examining Chase over the top of his spectacles. Chase had gone through a moment of panic, until he remembered that his departure on the morrow would postpone this ordeal. But it remained uncomfortably with him. He had seen his tenants at the funeral, and had eyed them surreptitiously when he thought they

were not noticing him. They were all farmers, big, heavy, kindly
men, whose manner had adopted little Chase into the shelter of an
interested benevolence. He had liked them; distinctly he had liked
them. But to call upon them in their homes, to intrude upon their
privacy—he who of all men had a wilting horror of intrusion, that
was another matter.

He enjoyed being alone himself; he had a real taste for solitude,
and luxuriated now in his days and particularly his evenings at
Blackboys, when he sat over the fire, stirring the great heap of soft
grey ashes with the poker, the ashes that were never cleared away;
he liked the woolly thud when the poker dropped among them.
Those evenings were pleasant to him; pleasant and new, though
sometimes he felt that in spite of their novelty they had been always
a part of his life. Moreover he had a companion, for Thane, the
greyhound, slim and fawn-coloured, lay by the fire asleep, with his
nose along his paws.

There existed in his mind a curious confusion in regard to his
tenants, a confusion quite childish, but which carried with it a sort of
terror. It dated from the day when, for want of something better to
do, he had turned over some legal papers left behind by Nutley, and
the dignity of his manor had disclosed itself to him in all the
brocaded stiffness of its ancient ritual and phraseology. He had
laughed; he could not help laughing; but he had been impressed and
even a little awed. The weight of legend seemed to lie suddenly
heavy upon his shoulders, and he had gazed at his own hands, as
though he expected to see them mysteriously loaded with rough
hierarchical rings. Vested in him, all this antiquity and surviving
ceremonial! He read again the almost incomprehensible words that
had first caught his eye, scraps here and there as he turned the pages.
"There are three teams in demesne, 31 villains, with 14 bordars, i.e.,
the class who should not pay live heriot. The furrow-long measures
40 roods, i.e., 40 lengths of the Ox-goad of 166 feet, a rod just long
enough to lie along the yokes of the first three pair of Oxen, and let
the ploughman thrust with the point at either flank of either the sod
ox or the sward ox. Such a strip four rods in width gives an acre."
"There is wood of 75 Hogs. The Hogs must be panage Hogs, one in
seven, paid each year for the right to feed the herd in the Lord of the
Manor's wooded wastes."

What on earth were panage hogs, to which apparently he was entitled?

He read again, "The quantum of liberty of person and alienation originally enjoyed by those now represented by the Free Tenants of the Manor is a matter for argument for the theorists. The free tenants were *liberi homines* within the statute *Quia Emptores Terrarum*, and as such from 1289 could sell their holdings to whomsoever they would, without the Lord's licence, still less without surrender or admittance, saving always the condition that the feoffee do hold of the same Lord as feoffor. And the feoffee must hold, i.e., must acknowledge that he hold. There must be tenure in fact and the Lord must know his new tenant as such. Some privity must be established. The new tenant must do fealty and say 'I hold of you, the Lord.' An alienation without such acknowledgement is not good against the Lord."

He laid down the papers. Could such things be actualities? This must be the copy of some old record he had got hold of. But no; he turned back to the first page and found the date of the previous year. It appalled him to think that since such things had happened to his aunt, they were also liable to happen to him. What would he do with a panage hog, supposing one were driven up to the front door? Still less would he know what to do if one of those farmers he had seen at the funeral were to say to him, "I hold of you, the Lord."

Then he remembered that he had not found the people in the village alarming. He remembered a conversation he had had the day before, with a man and his wife, as he leaned over the gate that led into their little garden. On either side of the tiled path running up to the cottage door were broad beds filled with a jumble of flowers— pansies, lupins, tulips, honesty, sweet-rocket, and bright fragile poppies.

"Lovely show of flowers you have there," he had said tentatively to a woman in an apron, who stood inside the gate, knitting.

"It's like that all the summer," she replied, "my husband's very proud of his garden, he is. But we're under notice to quit." She spoke with an unfamiliar broad accent and a burr, that had prompted Chase to say:

"You're not from these parts?"

"No, sir, I'm from Sussex. It's not a wonderful great matter of distance. I'm wanting my man to come back with me, and settle near my old home, but he says he was born in Kent and in Kent he'll die."

"That's right," approved the man who had come up. "I don't hold with folk leaving their own county. It's like sheep—take sheep away from their own parts, and they don't do near so well. Oxfordshire don't do on Romney Marsh, and Romney Marsh don't do in Oxfordshire." He was ramming tobacco into his pipe, but broke off to pull a seedling of groundsel out from among his pinks. He crushed it together and put it carefully into his pocket. "I made this garden," he resumed, "carried the mould home on my back evening after evening, and sent the kids out with bodges for road-scrapings, till you couldn't beat my soil, sir, not in this village, nor my flowers either, but I'm under notice, and sooner than let them pass to a stranger I'll put my bagginhook through the roots of every plant amongst them," he said, and spat.

"Twenty-five years we've lived in this cottage, and brought up ten children," said the woman.

"The cottage is to come down, and make room for a building site, so Mr. Nutley told us," the man continued.

"We'd papered and whitewashed it ourselves," said the woman.

"I laid them tiles, sir, me and my eldest boy," said the man, pointing with the stem of his pipe down at the path; "rare job it was. There wasn't no garden, not when I came here."

"Twenty-five years ago," said the woman.

They both stared mournfully at Chase.

"I'm under notice to quit, too, you know," said Chase, rather embarrassed, as though they had brought a gentle reproof against him, trying to excuse himself by this joke.

"I know that, sir; we're sorry," the man had said instantly.

(Sorry. They had never seen him before, yet they were sorry).

"Miss Chase, your aunt, sir, liked my garden properly," said the man. "She'd stop here always, in her pony-chaise, and have a look at my flowers. She'd say to me, chaffing-like, 'You've a better show than me, Jakes.' But she didn't like peonies. I had a fine clump of peonies and she made me dig it up. Lord, she was a tartar—saving your presence, sir. But a good heart, so nobody took no notice. But peonies—no, she wouldn't have peonies at any price."

"There's few folks in this village ever thought to see Blackboys in other hands than Chase's," said the woman. "'Tis the peacocks will be grieved—dear! dear!"

"The peacocks?" Chase had repeated.

"Folks about here do say, the peacocks'll die off when Blackboys goes from Chase's hands," said the man. "They be terrible hard on a garden, though, do be peacocks," he had said further, meticulously removing another weed from among his pinks.

V

That had been an experience to Chase, a milestone on his road. He was to experience much the same sensation when his lands received him. It was a new world to him—new because it was so old— ancient and sober according to the laws of nature. There was here a rhythm which no flurry could disturb. The seasons ordained, and men lived close up against the rulings so prescribed, close up against the austere laws, at once the masters and the subjects of the land that served them and that they as loyally served. Chase perceived his mistake; he perceived it with surprise and a certain reverence. Because the laws were unalterable they were not necessarily stagnant. They were of a solemn order, not arbitrarily framed or admitting of variation according to the caprice of mankind. In the place of stagnation, he recognized stability. And as his vision widened he saw that the house fused very graciously with the trees, the meadows, and the hills, grown there in place no less than they, a part of the secular tradition. He reconsidered even the pictures, not as the representation of meaningless ghosts, but as men and women whose blood had gone to the making of that now in his own veins. It was the land, the farms, the rick-yards, the sown, the fallow, that taught him this wisdom. He learnt it slowly, and without knowing that he learnt. He absorbed it in the company of men such as he had never previously known, and who treated him as he had never before been treated—not with deference only, which would have confused him, but with a paternal kindliness, a quiet familiarity, an acquaintance immediately linked by virtue of tradition. To them, he, the clerk of Wolverhampton, was, quite simply, Chase of Blackboys. He came to value the smile in their eyes, when they looked at him, as a caress.

VI

When Nutley came again, a fortnight after the funeral, to his surprise he met Chase in the park with Thane, the greyhound, at his heels.

"Good gracious," he said, "I thought you were in Wolver-hampton."

"So I was. I thought I'd come back to see how things were going on. I arrived two days ago."

"But I saw Fortune last week, and he never mentioned your coming," pursued Mr. Nutley, mystified.

"No, I daresay he didn't; in point of fact, he knew nothing about it until I turned up here."

"What, you didn't let the servants know?"

"No, I didn't," Chase entered suddenly upon a definite dislike of Mr. Nutley. He felt a relief as soon as he had realized it; he felt more settled and definite in his mind, cleared of the cobwebs of a vague uneasiness. Nutley was too inquisitorial, too managing altogether. Blackboys was his own to come to, if he chose. Still his own—for another month.

"What on earth have you got there?" said Nutley peering at a crumpled bunch that Chase carried in his hand.

"Butcher-boys," replied Chase.

"They're wild orchids," said Mr. Nutley, after peering a little closer. "Why do you call them butcher-boys?"

"That's what the children call them," mumbled Chase, "I don't know them by any other name. Ugly things, anyhow," he added, flinging them away.

"Soft, soft," said Nutley to himself, tapping his forehead as he walked on alone.

He proceeded towards the house. Queer of Chase, to come back like that, without a word to anyone. What about that business of his in Wolverhampton? He seemed to be less anxious about that now. As though he couldn't leave matters to Nutley and Farebrother, Solicitors and Estate Agents, without slipping back to see to things himself! Spying, no less. Queer, sly, silent fellow, mooning about the park, carrying wild orchids. "Butcher-boys", he had called them. What children had he been consorting with, to learn that country name? There had been an odd look in his eye, too, when Nutley had come upon him, as though he were vexed at being seen, and would have liked to slink off in the opposite direction. Queer, too, that he should have made no reference to the approaching sale. He might at least have asked whether the estate office had received any private applications. But Nutley had already noticed that he took very little interest in the subject of the sale. An unsatisfactory employer, except in so far as he never interfered; it was unsatisfactory never to know whether one's employer approved of what was being done or not.

And under his irritability was another grievance; the suspicion that Chase was a dark horse. The solicitor had always marked down Blackboys as a ripe plum to fall into his hands when old Miss Chase died—obstinate, opinionated, old Phillida Chase. He had never considered the heir at all. It was almost as though he looked upon himself as the heir—the impatient heir, hostile and vindictive towards the coveted inheritance.

Nutley reached the house, where, his hand upon the latch of the little wooden gate, he was checked by a padlock within the hasp. He was irritated, and shook the latch roughly. He thought that the quiet house, safe behind its gate and its sleeping moat, smiled and mocked him. Then, more sensibly, he pulled the bell beside the gate, and waited till the tinkle inside the house brought Fortune hurrying to open.

"What's this affair, eh, Fortune?" said Nutley with false good-humour, pointing to the padlock.

"The padlock, sir? That's there by Mr. Chase's orders," replied Fortune demurely.

"Mr. Chase's orders?" repeated Mr. Nutley, not believing his own ears.

"Mr. Chase has been very much annoyed, sir, by motoring parties coming to look over the house, and making free of the place."

"But they may have been intending purchasers!" Mr. Nutley almost shrieked, touched upon the raw.

"Yes, sir, they all had orders to view. All except one party, that is, that came yesterday. Mr. Chase turned *them* away, sir."

"Turned them away?"

"Yes, sir. They came in a big car. Mr. Chase talked to them himself, over the gate. He had the key in his pocket. No, sir, he wouldn't unlock it. He said that if they wanted to buy the house they would have the opportunity of doing so at the auction. Yes, sir, they seemed considerably annoyed. They said they had come from London on purpose. They said they should have thought that if anyone had a house to sell, he would have been only too glad to show parties over it, order or no order, they said, especially if the house was so unsaleable, two hours by train from London and not up to date in any way. Mr. Chase said, very curt-like, that if they wanted an up-to-date house, Blackboys was not likely to suit them. He just lifted his cap, and wished them good-evening, and came back by himself into the house, with the key still in his pocket, and the car drove away. Very insolent sort of people they were, sir, I must say."

Fortune delivered himself of this recital in a tone that was a strange compound of respect, reticence, and a secret relish. During its telling he had followed Mr. Nutley's progress into the house, until they arrived in the panelled library where the coral-coloured tulips reared themselves so luminously against the sobriety of the books and of the oak. Mr. Nutley noticed them, because it was easier to pass a comment on a bowl of flowers than upon Chase's inexplicable behaviour.

"Yes, sir, very pretty; Mr. Chase puts them there," said Fortune, with the satisfaction of one who adds a final touch to a suggestive sketch.

"Shouldn't have thought he'd ever looked at a flower in his life," muttered Nutley.

He deposited his bag on the table, and turned to the butler.

"Quite between you and me, Fortune, what you tell me surprises me very much—about the visiting parties, I mean. And the padlock. Um—the padlock. I always thought Mr. Chase very *quiet*; but you don't, do you, think him *soft*?"

Fortune knew that Nutley enjoyed saying that. He remembered

how he had caught Chase, the day before, studying bumbledories on the low garden wall; but he withheld the bumbledories from Mr. Nutley.

"It wouldn't be unnatural, sir," he submitted, "if Mr. Chase had a feeling about Blackboys being in the market?"

"Feeling? Pooh!" said Mr. Nutley. He said "Pooh!" again to reassure himself, because he knew that Fortune, sentimental and shrewd, had hit the nail on the head. "He'd never set eyes on Blackboys until three weeks ago. Besides, what could he do with the place except put it in the market? Tell me that! Absurd!"

He was sorting papers out of his black bag. Their neat stiffness gave him the reassuring sense of being here among matters which he competently understood. This was his province. He would have said, had he been asked a day earlier, that it was Chase's province too. Now he was not so sure.

"Sentimentality!" he snorted. It was his most damning criticism.

Chase's pipe was lying on the table beside the tulips; he picked it up and regarded with a mixture of reproach and indignation. It reposed mutely in his hand.

"Ridiculous!" said Nutley, dashing it down again as though that settled the matter.

"The people round here have taken to him wonderful," put in Fortune.

Nutley looked sharply at him; he stood by the table, demure, grizzled, and perfectly respectful.

"Why, has he been round talking to the people?"

"A good deal, sir, among the tenants like. Wonderful how he gets on with them, for a city-bred man. I don't hold with city-breeding, myself. Will you be staying to luncheon, sir?"

"Yes," replied Mr. Nutley, preoccupied and profoundly suspicious.

VII

Suspicious of Chase, though he couldn't justify his suspicion. Tested even by the severity of the solicitor's standards, Chase's behaviour and conversation during luncheon were irreproachable. No sooner had he entered the house than he began briskly talking of business. Yet Nutley continued to eye him as one who beneath reasonable words and a bland demeanour nourishes a secret and a joke; a silent and deeply-buried understanding. He talked sedately enough, keeping to the subject even with a certain rigour—acreage, rents, building possibilities; and intelligent interest. Still, Nutley could have sworn there was irony in it. Irony from Chase? Weedy, irritable little man, Chase. Not to-day though; not irritable to-day. In a good temper. (Ironical?) Playing the host, sitting at the head of the refectory-table while Nutley sat at the side. Naturally. Very cordial, very open-handed with the port. Quite at home in the dining-room, ordering his dog to a corner; and in the library too, with his pipes and tobacco strewn about. How long ago was it, since Nutley was warning him not to slip on the polished boards?

Then a stroll around the garden, Chase with crumbs in his pocket for the peacocks. When they saw him, two or three hopped majestically down from the parapet, and came stalking towards him. Accustomed to crumbs evidently. "You haven't had them destroyed, then?" said Nutley, eyeing them with mistrust and disapproval, and Chase laughed without answering. Up the centre walk of the garden, and back by the herbaceous borders along the walls: lilac, wistaria, patches of tulips, colonies of iris. All the while Chase never deviated from the topic of selling. He pointed out the house, folded in the hollow down the gentle slope of the garden. "Not bad, for those who like it. Thirty thousand for the house, I think you said?" "Then why the devil," Nutley wanted to say, but refrained from saying, "do you turn away people who come in a big car?" They strolled down the slope, Chase breaking from the lilac bushes an armful of the heavy plumes.

He seemed to do it with an unknowing gesture, as though he couldn't keep his hands off flowers, and then to be embarrassed on discovering in his arms the wealth that he had gathered. It was as though he had kept an adequate guard over his tongue while allowing his gestures to escape him. He took Nutley round to the entrance, where the station cab was waiting, and unlocked the gate with the key he carried in his pocket.

"You go back to Wolverhampton tomorrow?" said Mr. Nutley, preparing to depart.

"That's it," replied Chase. Did he look sly, or didn't he?

"All the arrangements will be made by the end of next week," said Nutley severely.

"That's splendid!" replied Chase.

Nutley, as he was driven away, had a last glimpse of him, leaning still against the gate-post, vaguely holding the lilac.

VIII

Chase didn't go back to Wolverhampton. He knew that it was his duty to go, but he stayed on at Blackboys. Not only that, but he sent no letter or telegram in explanation of his continued absence. He simply stayed where he was, callous, and supremely happy. By no logic could he have justified his behaviour; by no effort of the imagination could he, a fortnight earlier, have conceived such behaviour as proceeding from his well-ordered creeds. He stayed on, through the early summer days that throughout all their hours preserved the clarity of dawn. Like a child strayed into the realms of delight, he was stupefied by the enchantment of sun and shadow. He remained for hours gazing in a silly beatitude at the large patches of sunlight that lay on the grass, at the depths of the shadows that melted into the profundity of the woods. In the mornings he woke early, and leaning at the open window gave himself over to the dews, to the young glinting sunshine, and to the birds. What a babble of birds! He couldn't distinguish their notes—only to the cuckoo, the wood-pigeon, and the distant crow of a cock could he put a name. The fluffy tits, blue and yellow, hopping among the apple-branches, were to him as nameless as they were lovely. He knew, theoretically, that the birds did sing when day was breaking; the marvellous thing was, not that they should be singing, but that he, Chase, should be awake and in the country to hear them sing. No one knew that he was awake, and he had all a shy man's pleasure in seclusion. No one knew what he was doing; no one was spying on him; he was quite free and unobserved in this clean-washed, untenanted, waking world. Down in the woods only the small animals and the birds were stirring. There was the rustle of a mouse under dead leaves. It was too early for even the farm-people to be about. Chase and the natural citizens between them had it all their own way. (Nutley wore a black coat and carried a black shiny bag, but Nutley knew nothing of the dawn.) Then he clothed himself, and, passing out of the house unperceived with Thane, since there was no one to perceive them, wandered in the sparkling fields. There was by now no angle from which he was not familiar with the house, whether he considered the dreamy roofs from the crest of the hill or the huddle of the murrey-coloured buildings from across the distance of the surrounding pastures. No thread of smoke rose slim and wavering from a chimney but he could trace it down to its hearthstone. No window glittered but he could name the room it lit. Nor was there any tenderness of light whose change he had not observed, whether of the morning, cool and fluty; or of the richer evening, profound and venerable, that sank upon the ruby brick-work, the glaucous moat, and the breasts of the peacocks in the garden; or of the ethereal moonlight, a secret that he kept, inviolate almost from himself, in the shyest recesses of his soul.

For at the centre of all was always the house, that mothered the farms and accepted the homage of the garden. The house was at the heart of all things; the cycle of husbandry might revolve—tillage to growth, and growth to harvest—more necessary, more permanent, perhaps, more urgent; but like a woman gracious, humorous, and dominant, the house remained quiet at the centre. To part the house and the lands, or to consider them as separate, would be no less than parting the soul and the body. The house *was* the soul; did contain and guard the soul as in a casket; the lands were England, Saxon as they could be, and if the house were at the heart of the land, then the soul of the house must indeed be at the heart and root of England, and, once arrived at the soul of the house, you might fairly claim to have pierced to the soul of England. Grave, gentle, encrusted with tradition, embossed with legend, simple and proud, ample and maternal. Not sensational. Not arresting. There was nothing about the house or the country to startle; it was, rather, a charm that enticed, insidious as a track through a wood, or a path lying across fields and curving away from sight over the skyline, leading the unwary wanderer deeper and deeper into the bosom of the country.

He knew the sharp smell of cut grass, and the wash of the dew round his ankles. He knew the honing of a scythe, the clang of a forge and the roaring of its bellows, the rasp of a saw cutting

through wood and the resinous scent of the sawdust. He knew the
tap of a woodpecker on a tree-trunk, and the midday murmur, most
amorous, most sleepy, of the pigeons among the beeches. He knew
the contented buzz of a bee as it closed down upon a flower, and the
bitter shrill of the grasshopper along the hedgerows. He knew the
squirt of milk jetting into the pails, and the drowsy stir in the byres.
He knew the marvellous brilliance of a petal in the sun, its fibrous
transparency, like the cornelian-coloured transparency of a woman's
fingers held over a strong light. He associated these sights, and the
infinitesimal small sounds composing the recurrent melody, with the
meals prepared for him, the salads and cold chicken, the draughts of
cider, and abundance of fresh humble fruit, until it seemed to him
that all senses were gratified severally and harmoniously, as well out
in the open as in the cool dusk within the house.

He liked to rap with his stick upon the door of a farm-house, and
to be admitted with a "Why! Mr. Chase!" by a smiling woman into
the passage, smelling of recent soap and water on the tiles; to be
ushered into the sitting-room, hideous, pretentious, and strangely
meaningless, furnished always with the cottage-piano, the Turkey
carpet, and the plant in a bright gilt basket-pot. The light in these
rooms always struck Chase as being particularly unmerciful. But he
learnt that he must sit patient, while the farmer was summoned, and
the rest of the household too, and sherry in a decanter and a couple
of glasses were produced from a sideboard, at whatever hour
Chase's visit might chance to fall, be it even at eight in the morning,
which it very often was. That lusty hospitality permitted no refusal
of the sherry, though Chase might have preferred, instead of the
burning stuff, a glass of fresh milk after his walk across the dews. He
must sit and sip the sherry, responding to the social efforts of the
farmer's wife and daughters (the latter always coy, always would be
up-to-date), while the farmer was content to leave this indoor
portion of the entertainment to his womenfolk, contributing nothing
himself but "Another glass, Mr. Chase?" or the offer of a cigar, and
the creak of his leather gaiters as he trod across the room. But
presently, Chase knew, when the conversation became really
impossibly stilted, he might without incivility suggest that he
mustn't keep the farmer any longer from his daily business, and,
after shaking hands all round with the ladies, might take his cap and

follow his host out into the yard, where men pitchforked the sodden litter out into the midden in the centre of the yard, and the slow cattle lurched one behind the other from the sheds, turning themselves unprompted in the familiar direction. Here, Chase might be certain he would not be embarrassed by having undue notice taken of him. The farmer here was a greater man than he. Chase liked to follow round meekly, and the more he was neglected the better he was pleased. Then he and the farmer together would tramp across the acres, silent for the most part, but inwardly contented, although when the farmer broke the silence it was only to grunt out some phrase of complaint, either at the poverty of that year's yield, or the dearth of abundance of rabbits, or to remark, kicking at a clod of loam, "Soggy, soggy! The land's not yet forgotten the rains we had in February," thus endowing the land with a personality actual and rancorous, more definite to Chase than the personalities of the yeomen, whom he could distinguish apart by their appearance perhaps, but certainly not by their opinions, their preoccupations, or their gestures. They were natural features rather than men—trees or boles, endowed with speech and movement indeed, but preserving the same unity, the same hodden unwieldiness, that was integral with the landscape. There was one old hedger in particular who, maundering over his business of lop and top, or grubbing among the ditches, had grown as gnarled and horny as an ancient root, and was scarcely distinguishable till you came right upon him, when his little brown dog flew out from the hedge and barked; and there was another chubby old man, a dealer in fruit, who drove about the country, a long ladder swaying out of the back of his cart. This old man was intimate with every orchard of the country-side, whether apple, cherry, damson, or plum, and could tell you the harvest gathered in bushel measures for any year within his memory; but although all fruits came within his province, the apples had his especial affection, and he never referred to them save by the personal pronouns, "Ah, Winter Queening," he would say, "she's a grand bearer," or "King of the Pippins, he's a fine fellow," and for Chase, whom he had taken under his protection, he would always produce some choice specimen from his pocket with a confidential air, although, as he never failed to observe, "May wasn't the time for apples." Let Mr. Chase only wait till the autumn—he would show him what a Ribston or a Blenheim ought to be; "But I shan't be here in the autumn, Caleb," Chase would say, and the old man would jerk his head sagely and reply as he whipped up the pony, "Trees with old roots isn't so easily thrown over," and in the parable that he only half understood Chase found an obscure comfort.

These were his lane-made friendships. He knew the man who cut withies by the brook; he knew the gang and the six great shining horses that dragged away the chained and fallen trees upon an enormous wain; he knew the boys who went after moorhen's eggs; he knew the kingfisher that was always ambushed somewhere near the bridge; he knew the cheery woman who had an idiot child, and a husband accursed of bees. "Bees? No, my husband couldn't never go near bees. He squashed up too many of them when he was a lad, and bees never forget. Squashed 'em up, *so*, in his hand. Just temper. Now if three bees stung him together he'd die. Oh, surely, Mr. Chase, sir. We went down into Sussex once, on a holiday, and the bees there knew him at once and were after him. Wonderful thing it is, the sense beasts have got. And memory! Beasts never forget, beasts don't."

And always there was the reference to the sale, and the regrets, that were never impertinent and never ruffled so much as the fringes of Chase's pride. The women were readier with these regrets than the men; they started off with unthinking sympathy, while the men shuffled and coughed, and traced with their toe the pattern of the carpet, but presently, when alone with Chase, took advantage of the women's prerogative in breaking the ice, to revive the subject; and always Chase, to get himself out of a conversation which he felt to be fraught with awkwardness—the awkwardness of reserved men trespassing upon the grounds of secret and personal feeling—would parry with his piteous jest of being himself under notice to quit.

IX

When the inventory men came, Chase suffered. They came with bags, ledgers, pencils; they were brisk and efficient, and Chase fled them from room to room. They soon put him down as oddly peevish, not knowing that they had committed the extreme offence of disturbing his dear privacy. In their eyes, after all, they were there as his employees, carrying out his orders. The foreman even went out of his way to be appreciative, "Nice lot of stuff you have there, sir," he said to Chase, when his glance first travelled over the dim velvets and gilt of the furniture in the long Gallery; "should do well under the hammer." Chase stood beside him, seeing the upholstered depths of velvets and damasks, like ripe fruits, heavily fringed and tasselled; the plaster-work of the diapered ceiling; the fairy-tale background of the tapestry, and the reflections of the cloudy mirrors. Into this room also he had put bowls of flowers, not knowing that the inventory men were coming so soon. "Nice lot of stuff you have here, sir," said the foreman.

Chase remembered how often, representing his insurance company, he had run a casual and assessing eye over other people's possessions.

The inventory men worked methodically through the house. Ground floor, staircase, landing, passage, first floor. Everything was ticketed and checked. Chase miserably avoided their hearty communicativeness. He skulked in the sitting-room downstairs, or, when he was driven out of that, took his cap and walked away from the house that surrounded him now with the grief of a wistful reproach. He knew that he would be well-advised to leave, yet he delayed from day to day; he suffered, but he stayed on, impotently watching the humbling and the desecration of the house. Then he took to going amongst the men when they were at their work, "What might be the value of a thing like this?" he would ask, tapping picture, cabinet, or chair with a contemptuous finger; and, when told, he would express surprise that anyone could be fool enough to pay such a price for an object so unserviceable, worm-eaten, or insecure. He would stand by, derisively sucking the top of his cane, while clerk and foreman checked and inscribed. Sometimes he would pick up some object just entered, a blue porcelain bowl, or whatever it might be, turn it over between his hands, examine it, and set it back on the window ledge with a shrug of the shoulders. There were no flowers in the rooms now, nor did he leave his pipes and tobacco littering the tables, but kept them hidden away in a drawer. There had been places, intimate to him, where he had grown accustomed to put his things, knowing he would find them there on his return; but he now broke himself of this weakness with a wrench. It hurt, and he was grim about it. In the evenings he sat solitary in a stiff room, without the companionship of those familiar things in their familiar niches. Towards Fortune his manner changed, and he appeared to take a pleasure in speaking callously, even harshly, of the forthcoming sale; but the old servant saw through him. When people came now to visit the house, he took them over every corner of it himself, deploring its lack of convenience, pointing out the easy remedy, and vaunting the advantage of its architectural perfection, "Quoted in every book on the subject," he would say, "a perfect specimen of domestic Elizabethan," (this phrase he had picked up from an article in an architectural journal), "complete in every detail, down to the window-fastenings; you wouldn't find another like it, in the length and breadth of England." The people to whom he said these things looked at him curiously; he spoke in a shrill, eager voice, and they thought he must be very anxious to sell. "Hard-up, no doubt," they said as they went away. Others said, "He probably belongs to a distant branch of the family, and doesn't care."

X

After the inventory men, the dealers. Cigars, paunches, check-waistcoats, signet-rings. Insolent plump hands thumbing the velvets; shiny lips pushed out in disparagement, while small eyes twinkled with concupiscence. Chase grew to know them well. Yet he taught himself to banter even with the dealers, to pretend his excessive boredom with the whole uncongenial business. He advertised his contempt for the possessions that circumstances had thrust on him; they could and should, he let it be understood, affect him solely through their marketable value. The house itself—he quoted Nutley, to the dealers not to the people who came in view—"Small rooms, dark passages, no bath-rooms, no electric light." He said these things often and loudly, and laughed after he had said them as though he had uttered a witticism. The dealers laughed with him, politely, but they thought him a little wild, and from time to time cast at him a glance of slight surprise.

All this while he sent no letter to Wolverhampton.

He got one letter from his office, a type-written letter, considerate and long-suffering, addressed to P. Chase, Esq., at the foot (he was accustomed to seeing himself referred to as "our Mr. Chase" by his firm—anyhow they hadn't ferreted out the Peregrine), suggesting that, although they quite understood that private affairs of importance were detaining him, he might perhaps for their guidance indicate an approximate date for his return. He reflected vaguely that they were treating him very decently; and dropped the letter into the wastepaper basket.

XI

He saw, however, that he would soon have to go. He clung on, but the sale was imminent; red and black posters appeared on all the cottages; and larger, redder, and blacker posters announced the sale, "By order of Peregrine Chase, Esq.," of "the unique collection of antique furniture, tapestries, pictures, and contents of the mansion," and in types of varying size detailed these contents, so that Chase could see, flaunting upon walls, trees, and gate-posts, when he wandered out, the soulless dates and the auctioneer's bombast that advertised for others the quality of his possessions.

An illustrated booklet was likewise published. Nutley gave him a copy. "This quite unique sixteenth century residence"; "the most original panelling and plaster-work"; "the moat and contemporary out-buildings"; "the old-world garden"—Chase fluttered over the pages, and rage seized him by the throat. "Nicely got up, don't you think?" Nutley said complacently.

Chase took the booklet away with him, up into the gallery. He always liked the gallery, because it was long, low, deserted, and so glowingly ornate; and more peaceful than any of the other rooms in the whole peaceful house. When he went there with the booklet in his hand that evening, he sat quite still for a time while the hush that his entrance had disturbed settled down again upon the room and its occupant. A latticed rectangle of deep gold lay across the boards, the last sunlight of the day. Chase turned over the leaves of the book. "The Oak Parlour, an apartment 20 ft. by 25 ft., partially panelled in linen-fold in a state of the finest preservation," was that his library? it couldn't be, so accurate, so precise? Why, the room was living! Through the windows one saw up the garden, and saw the peacocks perched on the low wall, one heard their cry as they flew up into the cedars for the night; and in the evening, in that room, the fir-cones crackled on the hearth, the dry wood kindled, and the room began to smell ever so slightly of the clean, acrid wood-smoke that never quite left it, but remained clinging even when the next day the windows were open and the warm breeze fanned into the room. He had known all that about it, although he hadn't known it was twenty foot by twenty-five. He hadn't known that the panelling against which he had been accustomed to set his bowl of coral tulips was called linen-fold.

He was an ignorant fellow; he hadn't known; he didn't know anything even now; the sooner he went back to Wolverhampton the better.

He turned over another page of the booklet. "The Great Staircase and Armorial Window, (cir. 1584) with coats-of-arms of the families of Chase, Dacre, Medlicott, and Cullinbroke,"—the window whose gaudiness always seemed to attract a peacock to parade in rivalry on the outer ledge, like the first day he had come to Blackboys; but why had they given everything such high-sounding names? The "Great Staircase," for instance; it was never called that, but only "the staircase," nor was it particularly great, only wide and polished and leisurely. He supposed Nutley was responsible, or was it Farebrother? Farebrother who was so kindly, and might have wanted to salve Chase's feelings by appealing to his vanity through the splendour of his property?

What a fool he was; of course, neither Nutley nor Farebrother gave a thought to his feelings, but only to the expediency of selling the house.

He turned the pages further. "The Long Gallery,"—here, at least, they had not tried to improve upon the usual name—"a spacious apartment running the whole length of the upper floor, 100 ft. by 30 ft. wide, sumptuously ornamented in the Italian style of the sixteenth century, with mullioned heraldic windows, overmantel of sculptured marble, rich plastered ceiling," here he raised his eyes and let them stray down the length of the gallery; the rectangle of sunlight had grown deeper and more luminous; the blocks of shadow in the corners had spread, the velvet chairs against the tapestry had merged and become yet more fruity; they were like split figs, like plums, like ripe mulberries; the colour of the room was as luxuriant as the spilling out of a cornucopia.

Chase became aware that Fortune was standing beside him.

"Mr. Nutley asked me to tell you, sir, that he couldn't wait any longer, but that he'll be here again to-morrow."

Chase blushed and stammered, as he always did when someone took him by surprise, and as he more particularly did when that someone happened to be one of his own servants. Then he saw tears standing in the old butler's eyes. He thought angrily to himself that the man was as soft-hearted as an old woman.

"Seen this little book, Fortune?" he inquired, holding it out towards him.

"Oh, sir!" exclaimed the butler, turning aside.

"Well, what's the matter? What's the matter?" said Chase, in his most irritable tone.

He got up and moved away. He went out into the garden, troubled and disquieted by the excessive tumult in his soul. He gazed down upon the mellow roofs and chimney, veiled in a haze of blue smoke; upon all the beauty that had given him peace and content; but far from deriving comfort now he felt himself provoked by a fresh anguish, impotent and yet rebellious, a weak fury, an irresolute insubordination. Schemes, that his practical sense told him were fantastically futile, kept dashing across his mind. He would tell Fortune to shut the door in everybody's face, more especially Nutley's. He would destroy the bridge across the moat. He would sulk inside his house, admitting no one; he and his house, alone, allied against rapacity. Fortune and the few other servants might desert him if they chose; he would cook for himself, he would dust, he would think it an honour to dust; and suddenly the contrast between the picture of himself with a duster in his hand, and of himself striking at the bridge with a pickaxe, caused him to laugh out loud, a laugh bitter and tormented, that could never have issued from his throat in the Wolverhampton days. He wished that he were back in those days, again the conscientious drudge, earning enough to keep himself in decent lodgings (not among brocades and fringes, or plumed and canopied beds, not in the midst of this midsummer loveliness, that laid the hands more gentle and more detaining than the hands of any woman about his heart, not this old dignity that touched his pride), and he stared down upon the roofs of the house lying cupped in its hollow, resentful of the vision that had thus opened out as though by treachery at a turning of his drab existence, yet unable to sustain a truly resentful or angry thought, by reason of the tenderness that melted him, and the mute plea of his inheritance, that, scorning any device more theatrical, quietly relied upon its simple beauty as its only mediator.

XII

Mr. Nutley was considerably relieved when he heard that Chase had gone back to Wolverhampton. From being negligible, Chase had lately become a slightly inconvenient presence at Blackboys; not that he ever criticized or interfered with the arrangements that Nutley made, but Nutley felt vaguely that he watched everything and registered internal comments; yes, although not a very sensitive chap, perhaps—he hadn't time for that—Nutley had become aware that very little eluded Chase's observation. It was odd, and rather annoying, that in spite of his taciturnity and his shy manner, Chase should so contrive to make himself felt. Any of the people on the estate, who had spoken with him more than once or twice, had a liking and a respect for him. Perhaps, Nutley consoled himself, it was thanks to tradition quite as much as to Chase's personality, and he permitted himself a little outburst against the tradition he hated, envied, and scorned.

Now that Chase had gone back to Wolverhampton, Nutley arrived more aggressively at Blackboys, rang the bell louder, made more demands on Fortune, and bustled everybody about the place.

The first time he came there in the owner's absence the dog met him in the hall, stretching himself as though just awakened from sleep, coming forward with his nails clicking on the boards.

"He misses his master," said Fortune compassionately.

Nutley thought, with discomfort, that the whole place missed Chase. There were traces of him everywhere—the obverse of his hand-writing on the pad of blotting-paper in the library, his stick in the hall, and some of his clothes in a pile on the bed in his bedroom.

"Yes, Mr. Chase left a good many of his things behind," said Fortune when consulted.

"When does he think he's coming back?—the sale takes place next week," grumbled Nutley.

It was nearly midsummer; the heat-haze wickered above the ground, and the garden was tumultuous with butterflies and flowers.

"It seems a pity to think of Mr. Chase missing all this fine weather," Fortune remarked.

Nutley had no affection whatever for Fortune; he possessed the knack of making remarks to which he could not reasonably take exception, but which contrived slightly to irritate him.

"I daresay he's getting the fine weather where he is," he replied curtly.

"Ah, but in towns it isn't the same thing; when he's got his own garden here, and all", said Fortune, not yielding to Nutley, who merely shrugged, and started talking about the sale in a sharp voice.

He was in his element, Chase once dismissed from his mind. He came up to Blackboys nearly every day, quite unnecessarily, giving every detail his attention, fawning upon anyone who seemed a likely purchaser for the house, gossiping with the dealers who now came in large numbers, and accepting their cigars with a "Well, I don't mind if I do—bit of a strain, you know, all this—the responsibility, and so on." He had the acquisitiveness of a magpie, for scraps of sale-room gossip. Dealers ticking off items in their catalogues, men in green baize aprons shifting furniture, the front door standing permanently open to all comers, were all a source of real gratification to him; while in the number of motors that waited under the shade of the trees he took a personal pride. He rubbed his hands with pleasure over the coming and going, and at the crunch of fresh wheels on the gravel. Chase's ridiculous little padlock on the wooden gate—there wasn't much trace of that now! Front door and back door were open, the summer breeze wandering gently between them and winnowing the shreds of straw that trailed about the hall, and in the passage beyond; and anyone who had finished inspecting the house might pass into the garden by the back door, to stroll up the central walk, till Nutley, looking out of an upper floor window, taking upon himself the whole credit, and full of a complacent satisfaction, thought that the place had the appearance of a garden party.

A country sale! It was one that would set two counties talking, one that would attract all the biggest swells from London

(Wertheimer, Durlacher, Duveen, Partridge, they had all been already, taking notes), such a collection didn't often come under the hammer—no, by jove, it didn't! and Nutley, reading for the fiftieth time the name "Nutley, Farebrother and Co., Estate Agents and Solicitors," at the foot of the poster, reflected how that name would gain in fame and lustre by the association. Not that Farebrother, not that Co., had been allowed many fingers in the pie; he, Nutley, had done it all; it was *his* show, *his* ewe-lamb; he would have snapped the head off anyone who had dared to claim a share, or scorned them with a single glance.

He wondered to whom the house itself would ultimately fall. He had received several offers for it, but none of them had reached the reserve figure of thirty thousand. The dealers, of course, would make a ring for the furniture, the tapestries, and the pictures, and would doubtless resell them to the new owner of the house at an outrageous profit. Nutley had his eye on a Brazilian as a very probable purchaser; not only had he called at the estate office himself for all possible particulars, but on a second occasion he had brought his son and his daughter with him, exotic birds brilliantly descending upon the country solicitor's office. They had come in a white Rolls-Royce, which had immediately compelled Nutley's disapproving respect; it had a negro chauffeur on the box, the silver statuette of a nymph with streaming hair on the bonnet, and a spray of orchids in a silver and crystal vase inside. The Brazilian himself was an unpretentious cattle magnate, with a quick, clipped manner, and a wrinkled face the colour of a coffee-bean; he might be the purveyor of dollars, but he wasn't the showy one; the ostentation of the family had passed into the children. These were in their early twenties, spoilt and fretful; the tyrants of their widowed father, who listened to all their remarks with an indulgent smile. Nutley, who had never in the whole of his life seen anything like them, tried to make himself believe that he couldn't decide which was the more offensive, but, secretly, he was much impressed. "Plenty of bounce, anyway," he reflected, observing the son, his pearl-grey suit over admirably waisted stays, his black hair swept back from his brow, and shining like the flanks of a wet seal, his lean hands weighted with fat platinum rings, his walk that slightly swayed, as though the syncopated rhythm of the plantations had passed for ever into his blood; and, observing him, the strangest shadow of envy passed across the shabby little solicitor in the presence of such lackadaisical youth . . . The daughter, more languid and more subtly insolent, so plump that she seemed everywhere cushioned: her tiny hands had no knuckles, but only dimples, and everything about her was round, from the single pearls on her fingers to the toe-caps of her patent leather shoes. Clearly the father had offered Blackboys to the pair as an additional toy. They were as taken with it as their deliberately unenthusiastic manner would permit them to betray; and Nutley guessed that sufficient sulks on the part of the daughter would quickly induce the widower to increase his offer of twenty-five thousand by the necessary five. Up to the present he had held firm, a business convention which Nutley was ready tacitly to accept. He had reported the visit to Chase, but Chase (the unaccountable) hadn't taken much interest. Since then he had seen the brother and sister several times wandering over the house and garden, and this he took to be a promising sign. The father he hadn't seen again, but that didn't distress him: the insolent pair were the ones who counted.

XIII

Only two days remained. Chase had sent for his clothes, and had enclosed a note for Nutley in his letter to Fortune: "Press of business" prevented him from returning to Blackboys, but he was content to leave everything in Nutley's hands, etc. Polite enough. Nutley read the note, standing in the gallery which had been cleared in preparation for the sale. (It was, he thought, a stroke of genius to hold the sale in the house itself—to display the furniture in its own surroundings, instead of in the dreary frame of an auction room. That would make very little difference to the dealers, of course, who knew the intrinsic value; but from the stray buyers, the amateurs who would be after the less important things, it might mean anything up to an extra 25 per cent.). He was alone in the gallery, for it was not yet ten o'clock, and he maliciously wondered what Chase's feelings would be if he could see the room now, the baize-covered tables on trestle legs, the auctioneer's desk and high chair, the rows of cane chairs arranged as though in a theatre, the choicest pieces of furniture grouped behind cords at the further end of the room, like animals awaiting slaughter in a pen. The little solicitor was from time to time startled by the stab of malice that thought of Chase evoked; he was startled now. He clapped his hand over his mouth—to suppress an ejaculation, or a grin?—and glanced round the gallery. It was empty but for the lean dog, who sat with his tail curled like a whip-lash round his haunches, and who might have come down out of the tapestry, gravely regarding Nutley. The lean dog, scenting disruption, had trailed about the house for days like a haunted soul, and Nutley had fallen into the habit of saying to him, with a jocularity oddly peppered by venom, "I'll put you into the sale as an extra item, spindle-shanks."

Dimly, it gratified him to insult Chase through Chase's dog.

People began to filter in. They wandered about, looking at things and consulting their catalogues; Nutley, who examined them stealthily and with as much self-consciousness as if he had been the owner, discriminated nicely between the *bona fide* buyers and those who came out of idle curiosity. (Chase had already recognized the mentality that seizes upon any pretext for penetrating into another man's house; if as far as his bedroom, so much the better.) Nutley might as well have returned to his office since here there was no longer anything for him to do, but he lingered, with the satisfaction of an impresario. Could he but have stood at the front door, to receive the people as the cars rolled up at intervals! Hospitable and welcoming phrases came springing to his lips, and his hands spread themselves urbanely, the palms outwards. No sharpness in his manner! None of the chilblained acerbity that kept him always on the defensive! Nothing but honey and suavity! "Walk in, walk in, ladies and gentlemen! No entrance fee in *my* peep show. Twenty years I had to wait for the old woman to die; I fixed my eye on her when she was sixty, but she clung on till she was over eighty; then she went. It's all in my hands now. Walk in, walk in, ladies and gentlemen; walk upstairs; the show's going to begin."

It was very warm. Really an exceptional summer. If the weather held for another two days, it would improve the attendance at the sale. London people would come (Nutley had the sudden idea of running a special). Even now, picnic parties were dotted about, under the trees beside their motors. No wonder that they were glad to exchange burning pavements against fresh grass for a day. Chase—Chase wouldn't like the litter they left. Bits of paper, bottles and tins. He wouldn't say anything; he never did; that was exactly what made him so disconcerting; but he would look, and his nose would curl. But Chase was safely away, while the picnics took place under his trees, and women in their light summer dresses strolled about in his garden and pointed with their parasols at his house. Nutley saw them from the windows. For the first time since he remembered the place, the parapet of the central walk was bare of peacocks; they had taken refuge indignantly in the cedars, where they could be heard screeching. He remembered Chase, feeding them with bits of bread from his pocket. He remembered old Miss

Chase, wagging her finger at him, and saying "Ah, Nutley" (she had always called him by his surname, like a man), "you want to deprive an old maid of her children; it's too bad of you!"

But the Chases were gone, both of them, and no Chases remained, but those who stared sadly from their frames, where they stood propped against the wall ready to be carried into the sale room.

XIV

June the twenty-first. The day of the Sale. Midsummer day. Nutley's day. He arrived early at the house, and met at the door Colonel Stanforth, who had walked across the park, and who considered the solicitor's umbrella with amusement. "Afraid it will rain, Nutley? Look at that blue sky, not a cloud, not even a white one." They entered the house together, Stanforth rubicund and large, Nutley noticeably spare in the black coat that enveloped him like a sheath. "Might be an undertaker's mute," Stanforth commented inwardly. "Isn't Farebrother coming up to-day?" he asked aloud. "Oh, yes, I daresay he'll look in later," Nutley answered, implying as clearly as possible by his tone that it was not of the slightest importance whether his partner looked in or not.

"Well, there aren't many people about yet," said Stanforth, rubbing his hands vigorously together. "What about your Brazilians, eh? Are they going to put in an appearance? Chase, I hear, is still in Wolverhampton."

"Yes," answered Nutley, "we shan't see much of *him*."

"Of course, there was no necessity for him to come, but it's odd of him to take so little interest, don't you think? Odd, I mean, as he seemed to like staying in the place, and to have got on so remarkably well with all the people around. Not that I saw anything of him when he was here. An unneighbourly sort of fellow, I should think. But to hear some of the people talk about him, by Gad, I was quite sorry he couldn't settle down here as squire."

"As you say, there was no necessity for him to come to the sale," said Nutley, frigidly ignoring the remainder of Stanforth's remarks.

"No, but if I'd been he, I don't think I could have kept away, all the same."

Nutley went off, saying he had things to see to. On the landing he met the butler with Thane slouching disconsolately after him.

"You'll see that that dog's shut up, Fortune," he snapped at him.

An air of suspense hung over everything. The sale was announced to begin at mid-day, because the London train arrived shortly after eleven, but before then the local attendance poured in, and many people drove up who had not previously been seen at the house, their business being with the lands or the farms: farmers in their gigs, tip-toeing awkwardly and apologetically on the polished boards of the hall while their horses were led away into the stable-yard, and there were many of the gentry too, who came in waggonettes or pony-traps. Nutley, watching and prying everywhere, observed the arrival of the latter with mixed feelings. On the one hand their presence increased the crush, but on the other hand he did not for a moment suppose they had come to buy. They came in families, shy and inclined to giggle and to herd together, squire and lady dressed almost similarly in tweed, and not differing much as to figure either, the sons very tall and slim, and slightly ashamed, the daughters rather taller and slimmer, in light muslins and large hats, all whispering together, half propitiatory, half on the defensive, and casting suspicious glances at everyone else. Amongst these groups Nutley discerned the young Brazilian, graceful as an antelope amongst cattle, and, going to the window, he saw the white Rolls-Royce silently manœuvring amongst the gigs and the waggonettes.

"Regular bean-feast, ain't it?" said Stanforth's voice behind him. "You ought to have had a merry-go-round and a gipsy booth, Nutley."

Nutley uncovered his teeth in a nervously polite smile. He looked at his watch, and decided that it was time the London motors began to arrive. Also the train was due. Most of those who came by train would have to walk from the station; it wasn't far across the village and down the avenue to the house. He could see the advance guard already, walking in batches of two and three. And there was Farebrother; silly old Farebrother, with his rosy face, and his big spectacles, and his woolly white curls under the broad hat. Not long to wait now. The auctioneer's men were at their posts; most of the chairs in the gallery were occupied, only the front rows being left empty owing to diffidence; the auctioneer himself, Mr. Webb, had arrived and stood talking to Colonel Stanforth, with an air of unconcern, on any topic other than the sale.

The farms and outlying portions were to be dealt with first, then the house and the contents of the house, then the park, and the building lots that had been carved out of the park and that were especially dear to Nutley. It would be a long sale, and probably an exciting one. He hoped there would be competition over the house. He knew that several agencies were after it, but thought that he would place his money on the Brazilian.

A continuous stir of movement and conversation filled the gallery. People came up to Nutley and asked him questions in whispers, and some of the big dealers nodded to him. Nearly all the men had their catalogues and pencils ready; some were reading the booklet. The Brazilian slipped into a prominent seat, accompanied by his solicitor. A quarter to twelve. The garden was deserted now, for everyone had crowded into the house. Five minutes to twelve. Mr. Webb climbed up into his high chair, adjusted his glasses, and began turning over some papers on the desk before him.

A message was brought to Nutley: Mr. Webb would be much obliged if he would remain at hand to answer any point that might be raised. Nutley was only too glad. He went and leant against the auctioneer's chair, at the back, and from there surveyed the whole length of the room. Rows of expectant people. People leaning against the walls and in the doorways. The gaitered farmers. The gentry. The dealers. The clerks and small fry. The men in green baize aprons. Such a crowd as the gallery had never seen.

"Lot 1, gentlemen . . ."

The sharp rap of the auctioneer's little ivory hammer, and the buzz in the room was stilled; throats were cleared, heads raised.

"Lot 1, gentlemen. Three cottages adjoining the station, with one acre of ground; coloured green on plan. What bids, gentlemen? Anyone start the bidding? Five hundred guineas? four hundred? Come, come, gentlemen, please," admonishing them, "we have a great deal to get through. I ask your kind co-operation."

Knocked down at seven hundred and fifty guineas. Nutley noted the sum in the margin of his catalogue. Webb was a capital auctioneer: he bustled folk, he chaffed them, he got them into a good temper, he made them laugh so that their purses laughed wide in company. He had a jolly round face, a twinkling eye, and a rose-bud in his button-hole. Five hundred and fifty for the next lot, two cottages; so far, so good.

"Now, gentlemen, we come to something a little more interesting: the farm-house and lands known as Orchards. An excellent house, and a particularly fine brew of ale kept there, too, as I happen to know—though that doesn't go with the house." (The audience laughed; it appreciated that kind of pleasantry.) "What offers, gentlemen? Two hundred acres of fine pasture and arable, ten acres of shaw, twenty acres of first-class fruit-trees . . ." "That's so, sir," from Chase's old apple-dealer friend at the back of the room, and heads were turned smilingly towards him. "There spoke the best authority in the county," cried the auctioneer, catching on to this, "as nice a little property as you could wish. I've a good mind to start the bidding myself. Fifty guineas—I'll put up fifty guineas. Who'll go one better?" The audience laughed again; Mr. Webb had a great reputation as a wag. Nutley caught sight of Farebrother's full-moon face at the back of the room, perfunctorily smiling.

The tenant began bidding for his own farm; he had been to Nutley to see whether a mortgage could be arranged, and Nutley knew the extent of his finances. The voice of the auctioneer followed the bidding monotonously up, "Two thousand guineas . . . two thousand two hundred . . . come, gentlemen, we're wasting time . . . two thousand five hundred . . ."

Knocked down to the farmer at three thousand five hundred guineas. A wink passed between Nutley and the purchaser: the place had not sold very well, but Nutley's firm would get a commission on the mortgage.

Lot 4. Jakes' cottage. Nutley remembered that Chase had once commented on Jakes' garden, and he remembered also that old Miss Chase used to favour Jakes and his flowers; he supposed sarcastically that it was hereditary among the Chases to favour Jakes. That same stab of malice came back to him, and this time it included Jakes: the man made himself ridiculous over his garden, carrying (as he boasted) soil and leaf-mould home for it for miles upon his back; that was all over now, and his cottage would first be sold as a building site and then pulled down.

He caught sight of Jakes, standing near a window, his every-day corduroy trousers tied as usual with string round the knees; he looked terribly embarrassed, and was swallowing hard; the Adam's apple in his throat moved visibly above his collar. He stood twisting his cap between his hands. Nutley derisively watched him, saying to himself that the fellow might be on the point of making a speech. Surely he wasn't going to bid, a working-man on perhaps forty shillings a week! Nutley was taken up and entertained by this idea, when a stir at the door distracted his attention; he glanced to see who the late-comer was, and perceived Chase.

XV

Chase entered hurriedly, and asked a question of a man standing by; he looked haggard and ill, but the answer to his question appeared to reassure him, and he slipped quietly to the chair that somebody offered him. Several people recognized him, and pointed him out to one another. Nutley stared, incredulous and indignant. Just like his sly ways again! Why take the trouble to write and say he was detained by press of business, when he had every intention of coming? Sly. Well, might he enjoy himself, listening to the sale of his house; Nutley, with an angry shrug, wished him joy.

Meanwhile Mr. Webb's voice, above him, continued to advocate Jakes' cottage, "either as a building site or as a tea-room, gentlemen; I needn't point out to you the advantages of either in the heart of a picturesque village on a well-frequented motor route. The garden's only a quarter of an acre, but you have seen it to-day on your way from the station; a perfect picture. What offers? Come! We're disposed to let this lot go cheap as the cottage is in need of repair. It's a real chance for somebody."

"One hundred guineas," called out a fat man, known to Nutley as the proprietor of an hotel in Eastbourne.

"And fifty," said Jakes in a trembling voice.

Nutley suppressed a cackle of laughter.

"And seventy-five," said the fat man, after glaring at Jakes.

"Two hundred," said Jakes.

Chase sat on the edge of his chair, twisting his fingers together and keeping his eyes fixed on Jakes. So the man was trying to save his garden!—and the flowers, through whose roots he said he would put a bagginhook sooner than let them pass to a stranger. Where did he imagine he could get the money, poor fool? The fat man was after the cottage for some commercial enterprise. What had the auctioneer suggested—a tea-room? That was it, without a doubt—a tea-room! A painted sign-board hanging out to attract motorists; little tin tables in the garden, perhaps, on summer evenings.

The fat man ran Jakes up to two hundred and fifty before Jakes began to falter. Something in the near region of two hundred and fifty was the limit, Chase guessed, to which his secret and inscrutable financial preparations would run. What plans had he made before coming, poor chap; what plans, full of a lamentable pathos, to meet the rivalry of those who might possibly have designs upon his tenement? Surely not very crafty plans, or very adequate? They had reached two hundred and seventy-five. Jakes was distressed; and to Nutley, scornfully watching, as to Chase, compassionately watching, and as to the auctioneer, impartially watching, it was clear that neither conscience nor prudence counselled him to go any further.

"Two hundred and seventy-five guineas are bid," said the voice of the auctioneer; "two hundred and seventy-five guineas,"—pause—"going, going . . ."

"Three hundred," brought out Jakes, upon whose forehead sweat was standing.

"And ten," said the fat man remorselessly.

Jakes shook his head as the auctioneer looked at him in inquiry.

"Three hundred and ten guineas *are* bid," said the auctioneer, "three hundred and ten guineas," his voice rising and trailing, "no more?—a little more, sir, come!" in persuasion to Jakes, who shook his head again. "Lot 4, gentlemen, going for the sum of three hundred and ten guineas, going, going, gone." The hammer came down with a sharp tap, and Mr. Webb leant across his desk to take the name and address of the purchaser.

Jakes began making his way out of the room. He had the shameful air of one who has failed before all men in the single audacity of his life-time. For him, Lot 4 had been the lot that must rivet everyone's attention; it had been not an episode but the apex. Chase saw him slink out, burdened by disgrace. It would be several hours before he regained the spirit to put the bagginhook through the flowers.

"Lot 5 . . ." Callous as Roman sports proceeding on the retreat of the conquered gladiator. Scatter sand on the blood! Chase sat on, dumbly listening, the auctioneer's voice and the rap of the hammer twanging, metallic, across the chords of his bursting head. He had surely been mad to come,—to expose himself to this pain, madder than poor Jakes, who at least came with a certain hope. What had brought him—his body felt curiously light; he knew only that he had slipped out of his lodgings at six that morning, had found his way into trains, his limbs performing the necessary actions for him, while his mind continued remote and fixed only upon the distant object towards which he was being rapidly carried. His house—during this miserable week in Wolverhampton, what had they been doing to his house?—perpetrating what infamy? Sitting in the train his mind glazed into that one concentration—Blackboys; he had wondered dimly whether he would indeed find the place where he had left it, among the trees, or whether he had dreamt it, under an enchantment; whether life in Wolverhampton—his office, his ledgers, his clerks, his lodgings—were not the only reality? Still his limbs, intelligent servants, had carried him over the difficulties of the cross-country journey, rendering him at the familiar station—a miracle. As he crossed the stile at the bend of the footpath—for he had taken the short cut across the fields from the station—he had come upon the house, he had heard his breath sob in his throat, and he had repressed the impulse to stretch out both his hands . . . With his eagerness his steps had quickened. It was the house, though not as he knew it. Not slumbrous. Not secluded. Carriages and motors under the trees, grooms and chauffeurs strolling about, idly staring. The house unveiled, prostituted; yes, it was like seeing one's mistress in a slave-market. He had bounded up the steps into the hall, where a handful of loafing men had quizzed him impertinently. The garden door opposite stood open, and he could see right up the garden; was puzzled, in passing, because he missed the peacocks parading the blazon of their spread tails. The familiarity of the proportions closed instantly round him. Wolverhampton receded; *this* was reality; *this* was home.

He had gone up the staircase, his head reeling with anger when he saw that the pictures had been taken down from their places, and stood propped along the walls of the upper passage, ticketed and numbered. He had madly resented this interference with his property. Then he had gone into the gallery, sick and blind, dazzled by the sight that met him there, as though he had come suddenly into too strong a light. He had assured himself at once that they had not yet reached the selling of the house. Still his—and he stumbled into a chair and assisted at the demolition of Jakes.

The windows were wide open; bees blundered in and out; the tops of the woods appeared, huge green pillows; above them the cloudless sky; Midsummer day. Where, then, was the sweet harmony of the house and garden that waited upon the lazy hours of such a day?—driven out by dust and strangers, the Long Gallery made dingy by rows of chairs, robbed of its own mellow furnishing, robbed of its silence by sharp voices; the violation of sanctuary. Chase sat with his fingers knotted together between his knees. Perhaps a score of people in that room knew him by sight; to the others he was an onlooker; to the ones who knew him, an owner hoping for a good price. They must know he was poor—the park fence was lichen-covered and broken down in many places; the road up to the house was overgrown with weeds. Poor—obliged to sell; the place, for all its beauty, betrayed its poverty. Only the farmers looked prosperous. (Those farmers must have prospered better than they ever admitted, for here was one of them buying-in at a most respectable figure the house and lands he rented.) His over-excited senses quietening down a little, he paid attention to the progress of the sale, finding there nothing but the same intolerable pain; the warmth of his secret memory stirred by the chill probe of the words he heard pronounced from the auctioneer's desk—"ten acres of fallow, known as Ten-Acre Field, with five acres, three roods, and two perches of wood, including a quantity of fine standing timber to the value of two hundred and fifty pounds"—he knew that wood; it was free of undergrowth, and the bare tree-trunks rose like columns straight out of a sea of bluebells: two hundred and fifty pounds' worth of standing timber. Walking in Ten-Acre Field outside the edge of that wood he had scared many a rabbit that vanished into the wood with a frisk of white tail, and had startled the rusty pheasants up into heavy flight.

Knocked down to the farmer who had just bought-in his farm.

He didn't much resent the fields and woods going to the farmers. If anyone other than himself must have them, let it be the yeomen by whom they were worked and understood. But the house—there was the rub, the anguish. Nutley had mentioned a Brazilian (Nutley's most casual word about the house, or a buyer for the house, had

remained indelibly stamped on Chase's mind.) He looked about
now, for the first time since he had come into the room, and
discovered Nutley leaning against the auctioneer's high chair, then
he discovered the young man who must certainly be the Brazilian in
question, and all the dread which had been hitherto, so to speak,
staved off, now smote him with its imminence as his eyes lighted on
the unfamiliar, insouciant face.

The new owner, lounging there, insufferable, graceful, waiting
without impatience, so insultingly unperturbed! Cool as a cucumber,
that young man, accustomed to find life full of a persevering
amiability. Chase made a movement to rise; he wanted to fly the
room, to escape an ordeal that appalled his soul, but his shyness held
him down: he could not create a sensation before so many people.
Enraged as he was by the weakness that caught him thus, and
prevented him from saving himself while there was still time, he yet
submitted, pinned to his chair, enduring such misery as made all his
previous grief sink to the level of mere discomfort. He yearned even
after hours that lay in the past, and that at the time of their being had
seemed to him, in all truth, sufficiently weighted; the hours he had
spent standing beside the dealers during their minute examination of
his possessions, while he wrung out his pitiable flippancies; then, in
those days, he had known that ultimately they would take their
leave, and that he would be left to turn back alone into his house,
greeted by the dog beating his tail against the legs of the furniture, as
pleased as his master; or the hour when, sitting in this very gallery
(how different then!), he had read through Nutley's offensive
booklet, and had not known whether it was chiefly anger or pain that
drove extravagant ideas of revolt across his mind; those hours by
comparison now appeared to him elysian—he had tasted then but
the froth on the cup of bitterness of which he now reached the dregs.

God, how quickly they were getting through the lots! Lot 14 was
already reached, and 16 was the house. Surely no soul could
withstand such pressure, but must crumble like a crushed shell?
When they actually reached Lot 16, when he heard the auctioneer
start off with his "Now, gentlemen . . ." what would he do then,
how would he behave? It was no longer shyness that held him, but
fascination, and a physical sickness that made his body clammy and
moist although he was shivering with cold. Fear must be like this,

and from his heart he pitied all those who were mortally afraid. He
noticed that several people were looking at him, amongst others
Nutley, and he thought that he must be losing control of his reason,
for it seemed to him that Nutley's face was yellow and pointed, and
was grinning at him with a squinting malevolence, an oblique
derision, altogether fantastic, and pushed up quite close to him,
although in reality Nutley was some way off. He put up his hand to
his forehead, and one or two people made an anxious movement
towards him, as though they thought he was going to faint. He
rejected them with a vague gesture, and at that moment heard the
auctioneer say, "Lot 16, gentlemen . . ."

XVI

There was a general stir in the room, of chairs being shifted, and legs uncrossed and recrossed. Mr. Webb gave a little cough, while he laid aside his catalogue in favour of the more elaborate booklet, which he opened on the desk in front of him, flattening down the pages with a precise hand. He drew himself up, took off his glasses, and tapped the booklet with them, surveying his audience. "As you know, ladies and gentlemen—as, in fact, this monograph, which you have all had in your hands, will have told you if you did not know it before—we have in Blackboys one of the most perfect examples of the Elizabethan manor-house in England. I don't think I need take up your time and my own by enlarging upon that, or by pointing out the historical and artistic value of the property about to be disposed of; I can safely leave the ancient building, and the monograph so ably prepared by my friend Mr. Nutley, to speak for themselves. It only remains for me to beg those intending to bid, to second my efforts in putting the sale through as quickly as possible, for we still have a large portion of the catalogue to deal with, and to bear in mind that a reserve figure of reasonable proportions has been placed upon the manor-house and surrounding grounds.—Lot 16, the manor-house known as Blackboys, the pleasure-grounds of eight acres, and one hundred and twenty-five acres of park land adjoining."

A short silence succeeded Mr. Webb's little speech. The Brazilian and his solicitor whispered together. The representatives of the various agencies looked at one another to see who would take the first step. Finally a voice said, "Eight thousand guineas."

"Come, come", smiled Mr. Webb.

"Nine thousand", said another voice.

"I told you, gentlemen, that a reasonable reserve had been placed upon this lot", said the auctioneer in a tone of restrained impatience, "and you must all of you be sufficiently acquainted with the standard of sale-room prices to know that that nine thousand guineas comes nowhere near a reasonable figure for a property such as the one we have now under consideration."

Thus rebuked, the man who had first spoken said, "All right—twelve thousand."

"And five hundred", said the second man.

"Sticky, sticky", murmured Nutley, shaking his head.

Still neither the Brazilian nor his solicitor made any sign. The agents were evidently unwilling to show their hands; then a little man began to bid on behalf of an American standing at his elbow: "Thirteen thousand guineas."

This stirred the agents, and between them all the bidding crackled up to eighteen thousand. Mr. Webb, judging that the American was probably good for twenty or twenty-five, and wishing to entice the Brazilian into competition, said in the same resigned tone, "I am unwilling to withdraw this lot, but I am afraid we cannot afford to waste time in this fashion."

"Make it twenty, sir", called out the American, "and let's get a move on."

"Thank you, sir," said Mr. Webb, in the midst of a laugh. "I am bid twenty thousand guineas for Lot 16, twenty thousand guineas *are* bid . . . and five hundred on my right . . . twenty-one thousand on my left . . . thank you again, sir: twenty-two thousand guineas. Twenty-two thousand guineas. Surely no one wishes to see this lot withdrawn? Twenty-two thousand guineas. And five hundred. And two hundred and fifty more. Twenty-two thousand seven hundred and fifty guineas . . ."

"Twenty-three thousand," said the solicitor who had come with the Brazilian.

People craned forward now to see and to hear. The Brazilian had been generally pointed out as the most likely buyer, and until he or his man took up the bidding it could be disregarded as preliminary. The small fry of the agents served to run it up into workable figures, after which it would certainly pass beyond them. The duel, it was guessed, would lie between the American and the Brazilian.

"Twenty-four thousand," called out one of the agents in a sort of dying flourish.

"And five hundred," said another, not to be outdone.

"Twenty-five thousand," said the Brazilian's solicitor.

"Twenty-five thousand guineas *are* bid," said the auctioneer. "Twenty-five thousand guineas. I am authorised by Mr. Nutley, the solicitor acting for this estate, to tell you . . ." he glanced down at Nutley, who nodded, ". . . to tell you that this sum had already been offered, and refused, at the estate office. If, therefore, no gentleman is willing to pass beyond twenty-five thousand guineas, I shall be compelled . . . and five hundred, thank you, sir. Twenty-five thousand five hundred guineas."

Most people present supposed that this sum came very near to being adequate, and a murmur to this effect passed up and down the room. People looked at Chase, who was as white as death and sat with his eye fixed upon the floor. The American, good-humouredly enough, was trying to take the measure of the unruffled young man; judging from the slight shrug he gave, he did not think he stood much chance, but nevertheless he called, "Keep the ball rolling. Two hundred and fifty more."

The room began to take sides, most preferring the straightforward vulgarity of the jolly American to the outlandishness of the young man, which baffled and put them ill at their ease. (Nutley found time to think that the youth of the neighbourhood would need some time before it recovered from the influence of that young man, even if he were to pass away with the day.) Those who had the habit of sale-rooms thought Chase lucky in having two men, both keen, against one another to run up a high price. They bent forward with their elbows on their knees and their chins in their hands, to listen.

"And two hundred and fifty more," capped the solicitor.

"Twenty-six thousand guineas are bid," said Mr. Webb, who by now was leaning well over his desk and whose glances kept travelling sharply between the rivals. He was sure that the Brazilian intended, if necessary, to go to thirty thousand.

"Twenty-seven," said the American, recklessly.

"Twenty-eight," said the solicitor after a word with his employer.

The American shook his head; he was very jovial and friendly, and bore no malice. He laughed, but he shook his head.

"If that is your last word, gentlemen, I regret to say that the lot must be withdrawn, as the reserve has not been reached," said Mr. Webb. "I am sure that Mr. Nutley will pardon me the slight irregularity in giving you this information, under the exceptional circumstances . . ." Nutley assented; he greatly enjoyed being referred to, especially now in Chase's presence . . . . "I only do so in order to give you the chance of continuing should you wish . . ."

"All right, anything to make a running," said the American, who was certainly the favourite of the excited and eager audience; "two hundred and fifty better than the last bid."

The auctioneer caught the Brazilian's nod.

"I am bid twenty-eight thousand five hundred guineas . . . twenty-nine thousand," he added, as the American nodded to him.

"Thirty," said the Brazilian quietly.

He had not spoken before, and every gaze was turned upon him as, perfectly cool, he stood leaning against the wall in the bay of a window. He was undisturbed, from the sleekness of his head down to his immaculate shoes. He had all the assurance of one who is certain of having spoken the last word.

"I'm out of this," said the American.

"Thirty thousand guineas *are* bid," said the auctioneer; "for Lot 16 thirty thousand guineas. THIRTY THOUSAND GUINEAS," he enunciated; "going, for the sum of thirty thousand guineas, going, going . . ."

Chase tottered to his feet.

"Thirty-one thousand," he cried in a strangled voice, "thirty-one thousand!"

XVII

Of all the astonished people in that room, perhaps not the least
astonished was the auctioneer. He had never seen Chase before, and
naturally thought that he had to deal with an entirely new candidate.
He adjusted his glasses to stare at the solitary figure upright among
the rows of seated people, standing with a trembling hand still
outstretched. He had just time to notice with concern that Chase was
deathly pale, his face carved and hollowed, before habit reasserted
itself, and he checked the "gone!" that had almost left his lips, to
resume his chronicle of the bidding with "Thirty-one thousand
guineas . . . any advance on thirty-one thousand guineas?" and
cocked his eye at the Brazilian.

The Brazilian, equally surprised, had never before seen Chase
either. What was this fierce little man, who had shot up out of the
ground so turbulently to dispute his prize? He had not supposed that
it would be necessary to go beyond the thirty-thousand; nevertheless he was prepared to do so, and to make his determination clear he
continued with the bidding himself instead of leaving it to his
solicitor. "And five hundred," he said.

"Thirty-five thousand," said Chase.

The sensation he would have created by escaping from the room
half an hour earlier was nothing to the sensation he was creating
now. But he was exalted far beyond shyness or false shame. He
never noticed the excited flutter all over the room, or the extraordinary agitation of Nutley, who was saying "He's mad! he's mad!"
while frantically trying to attract the auctioneer's attention. Chase
was oblivious to all this. He stood, feeling himself inspired by some
divine breath, the room a blur before him, and a current of power,
quite indomitable, surging through his veins. Infatuation. Genius.

They must be like this. This certainty. This unmistakable purpose. This sudden clearing away of all irrelevant preoccupations. Vistas opened down into all the obscurities that had always shadowed and confused his brain: the secret was to find oneself, to know what one really wanted, what one really cared for, and to go for it straight. Wolverhampton? Moonshine! He was no longer pale, nor did he keep his eyes shamefully bent upon the ground; he was flushed, embattled; his nostrils dilated and working.

But everyone else thought him crazy, people sober watching the vaingloriousness of a man drunk. Even the auctioneer allowed an expression of surprise to cross his face, and varied his formula by saying suavely, "Did I understand you to say thirty-five thousand, sir? Thirty-five thousand guineas are bid."

Drunk. As a man drunk. Everything appeared smothered to his senses; intense, yet remote. His head light and swimming. Everything at a great distance. The crowd around him, stirring, murmurous, but meaningless. The auctioneer, perched up there, a diminutive figure, miles away. Voices, muffled but enormously significant, conveying threats, conveying combat. All leagued against him. This was battle; all the faces were hostile. Or so he imagined. He was glad of it. Fighting for his house? No, no! more, far more than that: fighting for the thing he loved. Fighting to shield from rape the thing he loved. Fighting alone; come to his senses in the very nick of time. Even at this moment, when he needed every wit he had ever had at his command, he found time for a deep inward thankfulness that the illumination had not come too late or altogether passed him by. In the nick of time it had come, and he had recognized it; recognized it for what it was, and seized hold of it, and now, triumphantly, drunkenly, was holding his own in the face of all this dismay and opposition. Moreover, they could not defeat him. Bidding in these outrageous sums that need never be paid over, he was possessed of an inexhaustible fortune. Undefeatable—what confidence that gave him! The more hands turned against him the better. He challenged everybody; he hardly knew what he was saying, only that he leapt up in thousands, and that in spite of their astonishment and fury they were powerless against him: there was nothing criminal or even illegal in his buying-in his own house if he wanted to.

And then the end, that came before he knew that it was imminent; the collapse of the Brazilian, whose expression had at last changed from deliberate indifference to real bad temper; the voice of the auctioneer, suavely asking for his name and his address; and his own voice, giving his name as though for the first time in his life he were not ashamed of it. And then Nutley, struggling across the room to him, snarling and yapping at him like a little enraged cur, quite vague and deprived of significance, but withal noisy, tiresome, and briefly perplexing; a Nutley disproportionately enraged, furiously gesticulating, spluttering at him, "Are you going to play this damned fool game with the rest of the sale?" and his answer—he supposed he had given answer, because of the announcement from the auctioneer's desk, which hushed the noisy room into sudden silence, "I have to inform you, gentlemen, that Lot 16, and the succeeding lots, which include the contents of the mansion, also the surrounding park, have been bought in, and that the sale is therefore at an end."

And, in the mist of his bewilderment, the sensation of having his hand sought for and wrung, while he gazed down into Mr. Farebrother's old rosy face and heard him say, half inarticulate with emotion, "I'm so glad, Mr. Chase, I congratulate you, I'm so glad, I'm so *glad*."

XVIII

Finally, the blessed peace and solitude, when the last stranger with the curious stare that was now common to them all had quitted the house, and the last motor had rolled away. Chase, leaning against a column of the porch, thought that thus must married lovers feel when after the confusion of their wedding they are at length left alone together. Certainly—with a wry twist to his lip—the events of the sale had tried him as sorely as any wedding. But here he was, having won, in possession, having driven away all that rabble; here he was in the warmth, and in the hush that sank back upon everything after the ceasing of all that hubbub; here he was left alone upon the field after that reckless victory. Poor? Yes, but he could work, he would manage; his poverty would not be bitter, it would be sweet. He suddenly stretched out his hands, and passionately laid them, palms flattened, against the bricks; bricks warm as their own rosiness with the sun they had drunk since morning.

Midsummer day. Swallows skimming after the insects above the moat. Their level wings almost grazed the water as they swooped. Midsummer day. All the mellowness of Blackboys, all the blood of the Chases, to culminate in this midsummer day. A marvellous summer. A persistently marvellous summer. He remembered the procession of days, the dawns and the dusks and the moon-bathed nights, that had hallowed his romance. He was inclined to believe that neither hatred nor its ugly kin could any longer find any place in his heart, which had been so uplifted and had seen so radiantly the flare of so many beacons lighting up the fields of wisdom. To cast off the slavery of the Wolverhamptons of this world. To know what one really wanted, what one really cared for, and to go for it straight. Wasn't that a good enough and simple enough working wisdom for a man to have attained? Simple enough, when it did nobody any harm—yet so few seemed to learn it.

Blackboys! Wolverhampton! What was Wolverhampton beside Blackboys? What was the promise of that mediocre ease beside the certainty of these exquisite privations? What was that drudgery beside this beauty, this pride, this Quixotism?

Thane gambolled out, fawning and leaping round Chase, as Fortune opened the door of the house.

"Will you be having dinner, sir," he asked demurely, "in the dining-room or in the garden this evening?"

THE END

VIRAGO MODERN CLASSICS

The first Virago Modern Classic, *Frost in May* by Antonia White, was published in 1978. It launched a list dedicated to the celebration of women writers and to the rediscovery and reprinting of their works. Its aim was, and is, to demonstrate the existence of a female tradition in fiction which is both enriching and enjoyable. The Leavisite notion of the 'Great Tradition', and the narrow, academic definition of a 'classic', has meant the neglect of a large number of interesting secondary works of fiction. In calling the series 'Modern Classics' we do not necessarily mean 'great' — although this is often the case. Published with new critical and biographical introductions, books are chosen for many reasons: sometimes for their importance in literary history; sometimes because they illuminate particular aspects of womens' lives, both personal and public. They may be classics of comedy or storytelling; their interest can be historical, feminist, political or literary.

Initially the Virago Modern Classics concentrated on English novels and short stories published in the early decades of this century. As the series has grown it has broadened to include works of fiction from different centuries, different countries, cultures and literary traditions. In 1984 the Victorian Classics were launched; there are separate lists of Irish, Scottish, European, American, Australian and other English-speaking countries; there are books written by Black women, by Catholic and Jewish women, and a few relevant novels by men. There is, too, a companion series of Non-Fiction Classics constituting biography, autobiography, travel, journalism, essays, poetry, letters and diaries.

By the end of 1988 over 300 titles will have been published in these two series, many of which have been suggested by our readers.

Also of interest by Vita Sackville-West
ALL PASSION SPENT*

"For a life of her own, he had substituted his life with its interests, or the lives of her children . . . It had never occurred to him that she might prefer simply to be herself"

In 1860, as an unmarried girl of seventeen, Lady Slane nurtures a secret, burning ambition—to become an artist. She becomes, instead, the wife of a great statesman, Henry, first Earl of Slane, and the mother of six children. Seventy years later, released by widowhood, she abandons the family home in Elm Park Gardens much to the dismay of her pompous sons and daughters. Retiring to a tiny house in Hampstead she recollects the dreams of youth, and enjoys the mellow present in the company of those she has chosen. There is her French maid Genoux, her house agent Mr Bucktrout, her painter and carpenter Mr Gosheron, and lastly Mr FitzGeorge, an eccentric millionaire who had met and loved her in India when she was young and very lovely. Lady Slane finds at last—in this world of her own—a passion, one that comes with the freedom to choose; this, her greatest gift, she passes on to the only one who can understand its value.

* As seen on BBC Television

THE EDWARDIANS

"These are the people, or a sample of them, who ordain the London season, glorify Ascot, make or unmake the fortune of small Continental watering-places, inspire envy, emulation; and snobbishness"

Sebastian and Viola, brother and sister, are children of the English aristocracy. Handsome and moody, at nineteen Sebastian is a duke and heir to the vast country estate, Chevron. A deep sense of tradition and love of the English countryside tie him to his inheritance, yet he loathes the glittering cold and extravagant society of which he is part. Viola, at sixteen, is more thoughtful, more independent: an unfashionable beauty who scorns every part of her inheritance, most particularly that of womanhood. It is July 1905, Chevron is once again the site of a lavish house party. The guests include Lady Roehampton, a great beauty and seductress, and the explorer Leonard Anquetil. It is Lady Roehampton who will initiate Sebastian in the art of love, but it is Anquetil, rough but humane, who opens for both brother and sister the gateway to another world.

FAMILY HISTORY

"For God's sake, leave me alone. Keep your friends, and leave me to mine! I'm too old for you, I belong to a different generation, I belong to the Jarrolds!"

Old Mr Jarrold is proud of the coal which has made his fortune; he is also proud of his daughter-in-law Evelyn, who has kept close to the heels of the family since her husband's death in the First World War, a caring mother to her son, Dan. At thirty-nine Evelyn is a woman of irreproachable conduct who parties and plays cards with the best of society. Then she meets Miles Vane-Merrick, a rising Labour politician, fifteen years her junior. Theirs is a love affair between people of different temperaments and different eras, for Evelyn knows only the social mores of her own circle and with Miles these securities dissolve. In this finely balanced novel, first published in 1932, the uncertainties of one relationship mirror the wider uncertainties of the 1930s, producing an elegant portrait of a country on the brink of change.

NO SIGNPOSTS IN THE SEA

"And now I see how I stand . . . I once flattered myself
that I was an adult man; I now perceive that I am
gloriously and adolescently silly . . . Geographically I do
not care and scarcely know where I am. There are no
signposts in the sea"

Edmund Carr is an eminent journalist and self-made
man. In middle age he learns he has only a short time to
live. Leaving his job on a Fleet Street paper, he takes a
passage on a ship to an unspecified destination—for
Edmund knows that Laura, a beautiful and intelligent
widow whom he secretly admires, will be a fellow-
passenger. Exhilarated by the changing colours of the
ocean and the distant tropical islands, Edmund strolls the
deck with Laura. This is a voyage of awakening. For in
these long purposeless days Edmund relinquishes the
past as he discovers the joys, and the pain, of a love he is
determined to conceal.